# Riverrun

# riverrun
## Peter Such

Illustrations by Shawnadithit

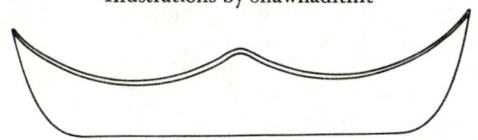

**CLARKE, IRWIN & COMPANY LIMITED**
**TORONTO/VANCOUVER**

© 1973 by Clarke, Irwin & Company Limited

Trade ISBN: 0-7720-1010-3
Education ISBN: 0-7720-1342-X

First printed in paperback format, 1975

*Canadian Cataloguing in Publication Data*
Such, Peter, 1939-
  Riverrun

ISBN 0-7720-1010-3 (trade pbk. ed.) —
ISBN 0-7720-1342-X (educ. pbk. ed.)

I. Title.
PS8587.U34R58   C813'.54   C74-2742-5
PR9199.3.S87R58

No part of this publication may be
reproduced or transmitted in any form or
by any means, electronic or mechanical,
including photocopy, recording or any
information storage or retrieval system
now known or to be invented, without
permission in writing from the publisher,
except by a reviewer who wishes to quote
brief passages in connection with a review
written for inclusion in a magazine,
newspaper or broadcast.

3 4 5 6   JD   85 84 83 82
Printed in Canada

To Nina and Ljuba, and to Helen Devereux,
Don MacLeod and Marian Hebb

and to
Harold Sonny Ladoo

# PREFACE

By 1800 the Beothuk population of Newfoundland had reached a critical point. Increased settlement had upset the delicate balance of their nomadic way of life and they were being indiscriminately slaughtered by the whites and their Micmac fur-trade allies, who were encroaching on Beothuk territory. Evidence suggests that about this time three or four hundred Beothuk were herded onto a point of land near their favourite sealing-site and shot down like deer. The memory of this slaughter persists among the present white population who call this place "Bloody Point" and the nearby stretch of water "Bloody Reach," names never found on any map. History books ignore the event but local traditions have been borne out by recent archaeological investigation indicating that the site was hastily abandoned at that time and never again revisited. The remaining Beothuk were reduced to hectic scavenging.

This novel has as its background the events of the next twenty-five years.

Very little is known about these Indians, the first inhabitants of North America to encounter Europeans. Peaceful but "intractable" (as one early explorer described them), they had a great skill in reworking iron—part of the evidence which suggests earlier Norse contact. For years, however, the Beothuk were confused by archaeologists with Naskapi and also Cape Dorset Eskimo, with whom they probably had friendly contact at sealing-sites and from whom they borrowed the toggling harpoon. Their use of red ochre, with which they smeared themselves liberally, led to their being called "Red Indians," a term that was later applied incorrectly to all the inhabitants of North America. Their peculiar language has proven to be a form of Algonkian—itself an old and widely distributed Indian language group in north-east

North America (see the work of Dr John Hewison of Memorial University). In fact, the Beothuk way of life and their use of red ochre suggest they may possibly have been the last remnant of the Archaic Indian tradition out of which many distinct tribes of North America evolved.

The unique ecology of Newfoundland could have contributed to this strange accident since the Beothuk's best adaptation to it meant staying as they were with only slight alterations. The island, which straddles several ecological zones, is known as an "ecotone" area—one which is impossible to categorize. Their highly unspecialized nomadic way of life was ideal for survival in an area where a number of food resources became available at various times of the year and at various places. Their "yearly round" from deep in the interior to the coast and back again was approximately three hundred miles. Newfoundland's separation from the mainland also prevented cultural interaction with other peoples on a large scale.

The chief and virtually only source of information about the Beothuk has been till now the sometimes contradictory but comprehensive compendium of documents and folklore published by J. P. Howley in 1915 after forty years of research. Archaeologically incorrect, it nevertheless contains nearly all the documentation available concerning confrontations between settlers and the Beothuk, including most of the fragments used in this novel. Newfoundland archivist Nimshaw Crewe has brought to light other archival material not contained in Howley (most important, the "Pulling" and "Liverpool" manuscripts). The diaries of John Peyton, Senior, key figure in the Beothuk story, were destroyed in recent years by his descendants.

My greatest debt is to Helen Devereux of Laurentian University. She not only allowed me to use her thesis in progress on the Beothuk, and site reports about her discoveries, but also directed me to helpful people such as Mrs Doug Woodman of Millertown, and John Moore of Grand Falls, Newfoundland. This information was supplemented by reports and observations made, while I was writing this novel, by my friend Donald MacLeod, Archaeologist for the Historical Sites Branch of the Ontario Government, and his colleagues, especially Jim Burns. Very valuable too were the researches of Dr James Tuck of Memorial University, through whose assistant archaeologists, Ray LeBlanc and Paul Carignan, I was able to visit sites being excavated.

There are many publications on related matters that I found helpful, especially those by Dr Edward Rogers of the Royal Ontario Museum, and bulletins published by the National Museum of Canada. Lastly I must mention the initial encouragement given to me by Dr Robert McGhee, now at Memorial, formerly Arctic Archaeologist for the National Museum of Man, Ottawa; Ron Evans, of the Ontario Arts Council; and David Blackwood, Newfoundland artist.

Financial assistance for my travels and researches in Newfoundland was provided by the Ontario Arts Council and the short-term grant facilities of the Canada Council.

It is tempting to explain my obsession with writing about the Beothuk. Let me just say it is a kind of debt I owe to Nonosabasut, Demasduit, Shawnadithit, Doodebewshet and Longnon—to whom I was introduced first through the pages of history—and to Osnahanut and the other persons in this book whom I met in dreams.

Peter Such

A way a lone a last a loved a long the

   riverrun, past Eve and Adam's, from swerve of shore to bend of bay

                        —James Joyce, *Finnegans Wake*

In the name of His Royal Highness the Prince Regent, acting in the name and on behalf of His Majesty King George III.

> PROCLAMATION
>
> WHEREAS, it is His Royal Highness the Prince Regent's gracious will and pleasure that every kindness should be shown and encouragement given to the native Indians of this island, to enter into habits of intercourse and trade with His Majesty's subjects, resident or frequenting this Government.—ALL PERSONS are therefore hereby enjoined and required, to aid by all such means as may be in their power, the furtherance of this His Royal Highness's Pleasure. Such as may hereafter meet with any of the said Indians inhabitants are especially called upon by a kind and amicable demeanour to invite and encourage communication, and otherwise to cultivate and improve friendly and familiar intercourse with this interesting people.—If any person shall succeed in establishing on a firm and settled footing an intercourse so much to be desired, he shall receive One hundred pounds as a reward for his meritorious services. But if any of His Majesty's subjects, contrary to the expression of these, His Royal Highness's commands, shall so far forget themselves, and be so lost to the sacred duties of Religion and Hospitality, as to exercise any cruelty, or be guilty of any illtreatment towards this inoffensive people, they may expect to be punished with the utmost rigour of the Law.
>
> Given under my hand at Fort Townshend Saint John's Newfoundland, this 10th. day of August 1813, in the fifty third year of His Majesty's Reign.
>
> (signed) R. G. Keats Governor.

# Nonosabasut

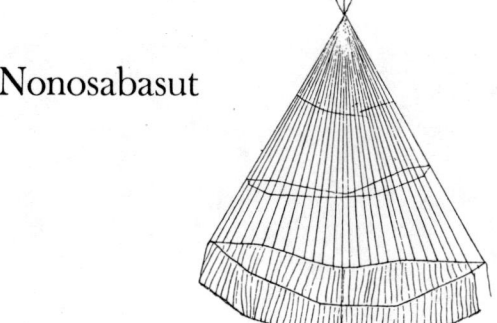

*September 1818*

This is where the riverrun ends. In the days of his childhood great sealfleets would congregate here, in this bay, a hundred canoes upturned on the cobbles, camping on their way to where gravel-bars between three islands out in the reach would glitter with seal-herds rolling and barking. But these last many years more and more whitemen have begun to tread the cobbles of this cove with heavy boots, to settle here in curious square houses and to build those long arms into the sea where their large ships can rest from the storms.

Watching from his clifftop birch Nonosabasut harbours the calm of this evening, at the calm turn of the tide, turn of the year into winter, turning point of his People's yearly journey to the sea. At first, Wothamisit the old story-teller would say, our People thought the whitemen's ships were bird-monsters. They were beaked and with wings like giant gulls they came walking over the waves. And from that day, he would say, this sea, which forever had borne the lifting easing canoes of the People out to the bird islands remained a part of the People no longer.

This evening the People will rouse themselves and move on. They will never return here again.

Nonosabasut shifts on the crook of the large silver birch and watches the last of the whitemen left on the beach chop into the last glint of fish on his splitting table. The man scrapes a last pile of offal onto the shingle then staggers with a last barrel, rolling it on edge to the wharf where he heaves and upends it onto the slippery pile in the wide boat's open belly.

In the last sun the whitemen's boat is full of eyes.

Safe now, onto the offal a gull-cloud descends. Yellow beaks and stony eyes: they scrap and scream until each has gorged his fill. Then, silent again they rise, they wheel, their thick wings reap the thin cool air and they settle, lilies, on the waves once more.

Ripples glow purple as the sky spills pink. Boatlines creak. The house-door slams and lights bloom in its windows.

Nonosabasut watches the last red embers of the sunset. His People are right to abandon this treacherous sea as his uncle Longnon has already done. The sea is part of the People no longer as Wothamisit says. The People must learn to rely only on their long deep lake, and on the speaking river that flows ten days' journey into this bay. As his uncle Longnon says, and Wothamisit too, the People must build up those other deerfences that have gone unused since the time of their grandfathers when the People were many and were untroubled before the great massacre by the whitemen at their sealing-place.

Full dark.

Nonosabasut again hears the house-door grate open.

A man with a swinging crystal fire dangling from his arm walks to the wharf's end. He inspects the boat. The eyes in the boat glint as his do when the light flickers into them. This is not the man who was last at the splitting-table. This is the oldman, their leader.

This is the cruel one who brought his trapping party up to Longnon's new settlement two seasons ago where Demasduit's mother, his own mother by marriage, had gone to live.

After the raid, Longnon had shown the People where Demasduit's mother, his own mother by marriage, still lay in the snowbank stained crimson. The river's water and the river's air were still that early spring. Stones apart, ants crawled on the crumbling riverbank. His own heart was beating anger as it beats within him now seeing this murderer. He heard the mourning keening of his wife Demasduit break the silence, and his own voice too and the rest of the People's voices. Their mother who had died stone lonely apart from the People, her blood let from her by the furriers' longknives. . . .

Knees locked Nonosabasut clings to the strong birchtrunk till his anger passes. The tree's skin is sweet. He'll never climb up it again. For three days it has borne him and the other watchers: Osnahanut, his marriage-brother and Shawnadithit, those two inseparables. The birch's trunk is decorated with red ochre stains from their hands and feet. The old tree nods a little as Nonosabasut clings to it in the beginning night wind. Subtle breakers begin their chorus on the shingle. Below him other trees stir. He listens. Yes. It is time.

Young Osnahanut is right. Before they launch upriver again never to return the People should take this whiteman's boat. That will let them know. This was once the People's place. Osnahanut is right. The whitemen's whole season's catch is in that boat, both fresh and dried. If the People strand it on one of the smaller islands its cargo will rot before they can find it. And its sails will make good covering for the People's winter mamateeks.

When he descends, his wife Demasduit is there and she greets him.

—Come, Nonosabasut. The People are eating. Waunathoake was crying for you again but she fell asleep in Shawnadithit's arms.

The worry for his daughter tightens his heart.
—Is she fretful again?
—I think she has a little fever but her cough seems better.

He holds Demasduit in the utter darkness of the forest. A pinesmell as the inland mist descends and wraps them. A late moon tonight. That will help. His body hungers to be moving. Yes. Take the boat. His feet accustom to softer ground as he follows Demasduit.

There's no path. They leap from treefall to treefall to boulder to clearspace. This side of the ridge there's no wind at all, no sound of the sea. They will never return. But maybe the birch will remember them. Unless the whitemen decide to cut it as they've done to all the tall pines in all the other places. . . .

The People have gathered, their fire small with redhot stones in it. Wothamisit lifts out one of the small stones, holding it between charring barkstrips. He heaves it into a small birchbark vessel of water. It spits. He leans over the steam, inhaling its vapours, old Wothamisit.

Nonosabasut eats salmon and some of the dried egg-pudding made after their long journey in fog to the bird-island. He drinks blueberry liquor then tells them
—Not just the kettles and pots and knives and the cording. Osnahanut is right, we should take the whole boat, strand it on the second small island past the large one over that way, where the brookmouth is.

Wothamisit coughs hard in the vapours. He wheezes
—Wait. Wait. I must speak to this.

They wait for Wothamisit to speak. He rubs his face his chest dry.

—Ah, Nonosabasut, you are a full man. It is Osnahanut alone who should have the privilege to speak as foolishly as old people like me because he is still young and excusable. Believe me brave ones there's too much danger in the taking of boats. These cruel ones will come angry after us, and maybe track us right up to our lake. Remember how they came searching for us years ago and we sat with their leader in our biggest mamateek? Remember how the hostages were exchanged and the whitemen left, following the brookmouth path? Then it was, as I have often recounted to you who are too young to remember, that one of our young men taken as hostages returned, you it was Nonosabasut. And Nonosabasut warned us how the treacherous whitemen were not going for presents for the People but were going for reinforcements to surprise us. I would act this story out for you but I am tired with this cough and besides it is against this taking of the boat that I wish to speak to you. For recall how Doodebewshet here, mother of Shawnadithit, was chosen to cut off the heads of the two hostages that no one had wished to kill because there was no honour in it. Doodebewshet, with grit still in her hair, still mourning her husband. And one of the hostages was a redhaired man. The People fled. And all winter they hid in the sprucetrees and watched in fear the whitemen finding the two heads stuck on poles near the place of their treachery. Take just what we need, Nonosabasut and Osnahanut. It's only the joking spirit of your father, Nonosabasut, that causes you to want this.

Osnahanut decides it is his reply that's called for. He stands to address old Wothamisit.

—Well. I'm not sure, much-loved Wothamisit, that I'm so foolish as you think. With the boat safely cut away we'll have more time to take everything we want with dignity, not like mice at night. And we'll be able to untangle the sails. They'll keep two or three mamateeks from the wind this winter. And Wothamisit's will be the first covered to keep the coughdemon from him, I promise you.

Shawnadithit agrees —Since that time, Wothamisit, no men have dared come up to our lake again. After all, they don't realize we're much fewer now than we were then. They won't risk their heads just for a boat.

After a while the People decide Osnahanut is right.

They will take this boat, especially since they might never come here again.

Nonosabasut, Osnahanut and Shawnadithit are brought the small canoe. Shawnadithit's pleased to go with her uncles, to be with Osnahanut. There's really only Osnahanut left to marry her. But he's her uncle. That's still not thought proper, even in these days when the People are so few.

They prepare themselves in the flaring light. Fish-flat, fish-silver, the folding canoe lies on its side ready for them. Since there will be three of them there will be no need to steady it with rocks.

They go the long way then break out onto shingle. They jam two sticks as thwarts across its raised gunwales to open the bark envelope, then punt out with their pointed oars, brunting surfheads balancing until it's deep enough to kneel and paddle. Sidling whaleback waves, edging treacherous cobblebeds, they go slowly. Careful Shawnadithit stands to hunt the wharf. She discerns it.

Just then a light blooms. It's the oldman again. He knows the People are camped near. Yesterday he saw their smoke, and today that red stain left by Osnahanut when he went exploring the tilts while the men were eating.

They crouch, still. The tide rolls them shoreward. Cobbles nudge their knees. Be careful. They hold fast with paddles, waiting. If he douses his lantern-fire he might see them.

He's uneasy. He's seeing shapes everywhere. Swinging his light he begins treading shingle towards them. His heavy boots crunch small stones. A crabshell snaps. He stops. Who's there? He sees it's the splitting table. He curses. SOME DAMN LAZY FOOL. He pulls it like a toboggan to the nearest tilt. Then he takes another turn about on the wharf. He senses them there but sees nothing. Nothing. He returns to his kitchen and the dark bundles of his sleeping men.

Now's the time. They push against the cobbles and drive hard for the wharf's end. Hurry. To its posts. Nonosabasut holds tight. Osnahanut clambers for its decking. . . .

Another light! Two men this time. Osnahanut drops back fast. Shawnadithit steadies them. No time to escape, they've got muskets. . . . Shawnadithit imitates the sea's hiss. HIDE! She pulls one end under, gropes upwards for the decking. Under the wharf they hold it, breathing their mouths wide open.

The two men check ropes.

LOOKS ALRIGHT DON'IT?

OLD MAN PEYTON 'E'S PROPER GOT A WIND UP 'E 'AS.

THEM RED DEVILS IS 'ERE, BOY. YOU MARK IT. THEY'S 'ERE ALRIGHT, BOY.

EARLY MORNIN', TIDE'LL RUN OUT AGIN. NEAR FULL NOW. AND A GOOD NOR'EASTER SHOULD BLOW 'ER FAIR 'ARD FOR ST JOHN'S IT LOOKS LIKE.

They leave the wharf and walk the beach and check the tiltdoors. Shawnadithit can see best. Into her hair Osnahanut breathes —Gone yet?

They go in the side door, contented.

The three of them wait. Arms ache holding the canoe under the wharf. Then without speaking they all decide at once and they are in the open under the boat's hull. Osnahanut scrambles in first. Then they are all there, heaving the canoe aboard, undoing the boat's lines, sliding large sweeps into rowlocks and pulling on the sweeps, bucking the moonless small tide-run, at its peak now, trying to make distance, musket-shot distance. They are just managing the covemouth, catching the cross-race into open water, safe, when a light flares on the pier again.

A regular watch, and lucky they just missed it. The whitemen know now the boat is stolen. The People will have to move out quickly. Long before daylight, and a hunt is made for them, maybe with dogs, as many times before.

The sky has broken here and there. More of a moon shines. Calm at the tide's turn. They help Shawnadithit into the canoe to warn the People. They ballast it with pots, kettles, and clothing from the covered-in bow, as well as some of the salmon. There's still the stern cuddy to be broken into after they beach.

—Meet us by the brookmouth near the second far island.

They watch her diminutive, toy doll, toy canoe. But she is alive as they are alive, and the web of their kindred stretches across the seamless sea between the islands' mysterious spaces. Shawnadithit is laughing, and they begin laughing, thinking of how the People will also be laughing.

Even old Wothamisit.

The boat safely beached, the next day the People swarm to unload it. The women are pleased with the cache of dried salmon and work making bundles to store through the winter. Osnahanut is flaunting the large heavy sails. No room in the canoes and portaging them will be difficult, but they quickly make rafts to tow behind them. Nonosabasut breaks into the cuddies. Clothes. And a waistcoat. That's for Old Wothamisit who puts it on proudly. And then there are guns.

The People are afraid when they see them. There is shot and the powder that smells of the devil. Leave them, says Wothamisit. This is the source of the whitemen's evil. But Nonosabasut remembers the roar of the guns at the massacre and thinks of the whitemen finding them and perhaps coming after the People to kill them. He holds one in his hand. Perhaps this one will one day kill him. He takes them out one by one.

Shawnadithit asks —what will you do with them?

He jams the barrel of the first into the crook of a tree —we will destroy them. Then with all his force and with others helping bends them. With stones smashes the wood of their stocks and leaves them in a pile of useless litter.

Nonosabasut is ALIVE in his forest. The People's forest is wet. Groundwood is spongy silver birchsticks. CRACK they break sometimes like an old woman's bones. Their silver skins slip off leaving wet red rotwood under his moccasins. His moccasins in the wet turn red. Red too his hands with red ochre. As he stumbles they stain silver birchtrunks he grabs onto, and his tread sinks often in breathing bellies of mossbanks.

An old black spruce hits at his blundering shoulders, clutches at his ankles, he trips.

—Let me go old mother, let go.

His voice drowns in soaked woods. Spiderwebs catch in his face. The old tree will net him if he isn't careful. Is it his partridge she wants? The last sleeping partridge he took from the old mother spruce's branches? Did that offend her?

His leg aching he twists free but the old spruce lashes his face as he rises to spite him. Careful with old women, don't offend them. Demasduit had warned him, *Better go back in that burial shelter and appease that old woman with this Nonosabasut or bad luck will dog you.*

Ah. Here is the place. That old spruce was guarding it.

He enters the dripping rockshelter and lays down his partridge. *Peace, old mother, here is your ointment to ease your bones.* Demasduit has given him grease mixed with ochre in a birchsewn dish. Yesterday he'd run in here from the rain and CRACK he'd stumbled onto the old woman's bones. A bad omen, Wothamisit had told him. You must go into the shelter again as is proper.

He stands waiting for his eyes to see her, afraid to

step further in case he breaks more of her. Debris from the rockface and leafmold half bury her. In leaf-green light he begins smoothing on Demasduit's mixture.

Her feet first. Three of her toes are missing and he isn't able to find many of her tiny footbones. She's been resting here long. Even old Wothamisit could remember no talk of her. Searching, he finds crumbles of bones in the gravelly soil. To his left is the long legbone he'd snapped rushing inside from the hard rain of yesterday. He rubs very carefully, setting those bones back together.

The woven basket of her hips is also broken. How many children did she build in there? When she lived the People were still lords of the bays.

When he touches it, her spine crumbles into pieces like counters used in the knuckle-game. Her palms face upwards and he smears her hands carefully. Then each of her loose ribs and the arch of her collarbone. Bones of her neck. . . .

At last he looks on her face. He speaks to her. In her damp shelter his voice echoes. A long time he is still and staring. Then his fingers trace her eyesockets, the lift of her cheek. Was she once beautiful?

Over her jaw he rubs Demasduit's mixture. Then her teeth and the place where her ears would have been, and where her nose would have been and where once her eyes. . . . Last her round gourd of skull where the sheen of her dark hair would have caught in a young man's throat as the young man would have gazed at her in some summertime beachplace washing and rubbing each other with ochre . . . ALIVE.

He steps out of the cave and goes carefully round the old sprucetree's circle. In the mist his own mouth makes he tightens the thongs holding the partridge over his shoulder. After those thick rains it is still too wet for biting flies. Maybe it will be an early end of them this year. A white moth blossoms on a black limb of the old tree.

He commands a space of alders. They hold arms up at him, palms of their hands towards him. He strides them. They lean easy away. His face still stings. That old black spruce. Why should she have wanted to hurt him? She has already laid black limbs down to the ground as these old trees do. Her tired hands resting palms up her fingers have already rooted (that is what tripped him). Now he sees how her children will be growing up quickly around her as the old woman whose bones he disturbed must have seen her own children. And in the circle of her spruce-children she too will die, leaving them room, as the old woman must have died. Years from now too the whitemen will cut down these children leaving their cliffside strewn and empty as the People have been left strewn and empty.

This morning Demasduit had teased him, clung to his back as he knelt tying up thongs. She laughed feeling his tall strength. Waunathoake, more than two seasons old, clung to his legs. He scooped her up too. But she was still fevered and cried at him, wanting her mother. Put her down.

The party was waiting for him outside with clubs made from treeroots. He pushed the entrance hides aside. *Come on, Nonosabasut. The rain is long over.* Demasduit stood by the birchbark mamateek. Just then a warm breath of sun came. *Look, Nonosabasut.* A rainbow. A few seconds it trembled like a painted shaman's robe over the islands but a wind blew it away and a grey mist settled again. Waunathoake stood beside her. Nonosabasut kissed her. Her small face was hot still. Demasduit asked him *Tie up my moccasins.* Then she placed hands on her slim belly, laughing and teasing. He knelt for her. *Is it true, Demasduit?* Her fingers traced his earlobes lightly. It was true.

This is the good season, rains before snows. The partridge swing and bump against him. They are tied neck to neck with deerthongs over his shoulders. He holds one at his hip. Warm, limp, slippery feathers. His fingers stain it red. He has large hands. The palms of his hands remember smooth shafts of the old woman's bones.

The bird's neck limp. Its head dangles like an ornament. Twelve he has caught so far. A few more days, a little more cold in the air, and the partridge would have been drowsier, easier to club off the low branches where they roosted and waited at this time of year for winter's changes to work inside them. But it wasn't a good thing to take too many. During the difficult springtime they might not come your way because the spirit who ruled them considered you greedy.

It was a lucky hunt. There were no birds at first. Then by the swamp he had found a foxtrack and they followed it. A short jog, and they found feathers on the ground. Not far now. Further along there were more remains. But two birds had been enough for the fox. Nonosabasut had shown his party where moss-pelts had been ripped off a boulder as the fox had skidded on it leaping a tangle of fallen birch on the way back to his den.

They rested. In the wet rotted birchwood were sweet ants. Young Osnahanut kicked them out and they each tasted a few while they chatted. *You are right, Nonosabasut, we should be pushing upriver starting tomorrow. The others will be needing help for the deerfences. In this strange weather who knows the caribou may come early and if the fences are not ready . . . .* Wothamisit spoke. *Why it was in the time of Osnahanut's grandfather, when the fences were not ready, the herd jumped up from the riverbank, and found the break in it. They were stampeding. They jostled each other. Their spreads tangled* CLACK CLACK *and some broke. Some were falling sideways like this. And we kill like this.* Then Wothamisit demonstrated. *Every man runs for himself.* THWOCK THWOCK THWOCK *his arrows.* Wothamisit's thin arms pulled his bowstring in excitement. *Aah!* His old man's quick mouth spat. *Disgusting! Five of the People wounded. Storehouses gone empty before even the otter cubs come. What a winter . . . .* Then Wothamisit sat again, coughed, spat again.

17

Then Osnahanut asked, *Nonosabasut, we saw you tying Demasduit's moccasins. Is it true she is building another baby?* He said *Yes, Osnahanut, it is true.* Osnahanut leapt three times for him.

From where the fox had turned Nonosabasut knew the birds would be roosting no more than one cliff-run away. From the top of the cliff they would be able to see down into the valley where they would be roosting. Only Wothamisit had been coughing as they travelled. But he was afraid to anger him by telling him *Go back Wothamisit, there is the hard trip upriver we cannot have you sick for.*

Sometimes the cough went away quickly this time of year. But if it did not go away after the first few caribou feasts, then the man would lie down in his family's mamateek close by his hearth as the first down snow fell on its sewn bark walls. And his wife and family would spend much time building a steamhut for him and tending him in the steamhut. Then one day the man wouldn't go into the steamhut no matter how his wife pleaded and cried. He would turn in his sleeping hollow and shiver and eat nothing and weep while they were rubbing his chest with warm grease. Then he would be silent and in the morning there would be his wife wailing and the People would bear his cold body out of the sleeping hollow, cover him with ochre and sew him in birchbark and bury him on a cliff facing west over the People's lake. If the ground was not too frozen by then. If the ground was frozen he would lie under the snow with the other asleep-dead things safe until the beach showed yellow again. And the sand would run free through the People's fingers.

There are too many the coughdemon is killing this year. Even in summer he is killing. He killed Wothamisit's grandson while the People were on the sea-islands. It had saddened Wothamisit and his own cough began soon after because of his sorrow. The boy had been growing well and his mother had made him a fringed deerskin suit he was proud of.

He, Nonosabasut, had carried the child's body into the cave and set it down near the boy's father that the People had laid there some six years before. This was Wothamisit's third son, the boy's father, who had been shot by a whiteman and died on the shingle.

With the boy the People placed small articles they had made. Toy canoes for the boy's spirit to float in, tiny bows and arrows for him to use, packages of ochre, and a parcel his mother had made of dried fish tied with rootstrings. After the ochre was put on everything, the boy was covered over with a beaver-robe that he used to sleep with. The boy's father had been placed on a ledge higher up. Wothamisit went in there to smear ochre on his third son's bones as he, Nonosabasut, had done the other day with the old woman. Next to his father, the boy looked like a toy, a miniature, because the boy's father was one of the tall men like Nonosabasut himself.

*There are not enough children,* Wothamisit had told him. *The People are fewer than when I was young. Then there were hundreds of mamateeks around the great lake in winter and another whole line of deerfences that would trap caribou. In those times the People had no trouble living all through the winters. And in the summers we could go round the coast down to the seal-place. But we cannot do that now, as you, Nonosabasut, know well.*

*I know that well, Wothamisit, and that's why I think the People should stay more together and make more of the salmon and be certain of the deerfences. Soon we shall have to leave the fresh sea-islands to the whitemen entirely and make our life only by the great lake and the great river all together.*

What he hadn't said to Wothamisit was, *When we grow strong, when there are many more hundreds of us, we must borrow the whiteman's tools and make peace with them like those cursed Micmacs who came in whiteman's boats and with whiteman's guns, crazy with whiteman's drink to destroy our westcoast People who had always met them before as friends and had shared with them.*

At the clifftop they looked down on the drowsy flocks of partridge. Then they went separate. Wothamisit was tired. He coughed several times more.

*Wothamisit, we will leave you this near side.*

Alone he, Nonosabasut, had culled the stony valley. How helpless these mute birds. Dried fish parcels, shapeless and separate, they hung in sprucetrees. The first turned quick eyes on him but his club was already swinging THUMP. It fell down.

He waited for the sound of another bird's startle that would send the flock winging. There was none. He crept up to another that was sleeping. An awkward angle. THUMP. This one fluttered and cried. Not hit right. His hand caught its neck. Squeeze. It grew still.

He is a good hunter. Even in those hunts like this one that took no courage. The forest respects Nonosabasut, Wothamisit tells everyone. But sometimes, returning with his dead prizes, he has the bad feeling of brutal moments, a haunting of fierce free eyes clouding with death, a wish within him to make some ceremony, some amends. Wothamisit told him there used to be a chant he learned as a boy that hunters would sing to the spirits of the hunted before setting out and again when they returned. But he had forgotten most of the words. There were many other small ceremonies that had been known to the shamans among the People, his own father as well. But such magic had all been forgotten when his father and the others had all died in the big massacre at the sealing-site.

He remembered those last days of his own father's life. His father had said, *Now you are ten years old, this summer you can come and see for yourself.* And that was the first time, at the sealing, he'd seen a horizon of skinned carcasses, soft boulders from the sea, piled where the white hunters had left them. Towards the season's end, he saw a beach again littered, but this time with the shot-down bodies of the People, his father's lost somewhere among them. It was only after his escape with Wothamisit that the sight had made him vomit and shake. Would the whitemen have skinned those carcasses also?

Since then he always grew sad after a large killing, whether of birds like today, or of the caribou that were coming soon.

Because he was ten, lithe and strong for his age, his father had decided to take him with him down the coast to meet with more large canoes than he could count at the place where the seal always came to be hunted. There were many tales of this place and what had happened there. His father had shown him some stone tools incredibly fine, that had washed out of the gravel beaches which strung together the sea-islands. These tools belonged to the far north hunters who first showed the People how to make clutching harpoon heads many generations ago. Submerged at high tide, the gravel beaches had been known to strand whales and other monsters. There were other tools, massive and black. These frightened him. His father told him, *We find these when the tide is far out. They cut our feet when we have to go wading there to bring up the carcasses. These belong to the race of giants who were the first People's ancestors.*

On their way there, in open water, they passed an ice-island. It was bigger than he'd imagined it from his father's tales of such things. By its edge, seal and dolphin seemed to run over firm waves like children. Light flashed from its cliffs as it did from the nine quartz crystals his father kept as treasures and sometimes allowed him to play with. The paddlers became cautious although they were still far away. Looking down into bright water he saw a white shelf looming there. Black darts of mackerel scattered from the canoe's shadow, like frantic spiders when an old mamateek is torn down with a shower of barkdust and old moss.

Their third day on the seacoast a squall caught them turning into a bay. The canoe bounced more than he'd ever known it to on the narrow lake where he'd always lived. Soon the moss on top of the stone ballast was wet under his knees. Rain pelted them. His father waved the paddlers to run before the waves into shore. But close to the shore he could see there wasn't any shingle. Waves broke over the gunwales, dashed on, and smashed to pieces at a high cliff's feet. The men began throwing out rocks, trusting to water for ballast. They slapped wavetops with their paddles, hoping to keep from tipping until they'd drifted further into the bay. Then through the rain he saw a place where the cliffwall broke. Up to their waists in water they pushed hard for the break. They spilled just before the beach.

He went under and under. One of the men grabbed his hair and hauled him gasping and stumbling through the freezing surf. Onto the shingle. Some brave ones pulled the canoe high to save it from battering. They emptied the rest of the boulder ballast and turned it upside down. A shelter. His father hugged him. His father sang a song of otters.

> *Bafu buth babashot*
> *Sieth o da banyish*
> *Eda ban see*
> *—Dosadöoosh—*
> *Eda ban seek . . . .*

That night was cold. But once rain stopped they peeled birchbark, tearing thin strips to make a large springy pile like cut white hair. They collected thin spruceboughs, also for the fire, and broke arm-thin birches between boulders, laying those sticks on top. Most of their parcels and bags were safe, being greased and ochred in case of a spill. His father found his hemispheres of iron pyrites and hammered them together till sparks ran along the edges of barkstrips and he could blow smoulders into flames. With a fire larger than usual they could fling on wet wood. It hiss-dried and ignited, bark spattering for a few moments, its flare carving sharply in the darkness the nearest faces.

Their talk that night was of old disasters. Under his damp sleep-robe he kept drowning in whirlpools of oldtime stories. Swimming up out of them he would start awake, panting, glad for the orange fire in its bright present, glad of his People's living faces, glad to shift his numbed hip round on spruceboughs springy and perfumed, just cut from living woods.

Then he would sink again into clutching tides of his People's history.

—Nonos-a-ba-sut! Nonos-a-ba-sut!

It's Osnahanut's voice. Nonosabasut calls back — Osna-ha-nut!

Osnahanut comes skidding on the sides of his feet down the cliff. He is cheerful.

—How many? How many did you kill? Show them to me, Nonosabasut.

He shows Osnahanut his twelve, laying them on a moss-bed. Osnahanut places his own string beside his marriage-brother's — Osnahanut has one bird more. He laughs.

—There! Nonosabasut, now who is the best hunter, eh? What do you say to that, brother?

But Nonosabasut has heard the breathing of Wothamisit in the spaces between Osnahanut's words, and hearing Osnahanut's words he knows, too, they are not his own words but someone else's. Not letting his eyes seek Wothamisit's hiding place, he addresses Osnahanut.

—Oh, Osnahanut, it is true, my brave little brother, I have long known what a hunter you are. Why, my brother, to keep my face I have often . . . well . . . let me not say this to your pure young heart directly. But can you imagine, my brother, that one of our family would even take another's catch to add to his own that he might appear more worthy?

Osnahanut is surprised. Then he laughs and turns and dances at the joke turned round on him. Then Wothamisit and the others leave their hiding-places and join in the laugh. Wothamisit's thin ribs heave. He splutters —Yes. Yes. The four I catch we give to Osnahanut for this joke. Ah Nonosabasut, your wit is like your singing father's. Hee hee hee. You . . . so much distracted, my thoughtful son . . . we keep behind you all this last way and put your brother up to it. Ah! Curse this wheeze! Oh. Oh. Ah. Aaah.

He falls. Seeing pain kill laughter in him the People gather up old Wothamisit. Nonosabasut captures the old man's spittle in his hand. He looks then dashes it upon a birchtrunk. Wothamisit is quiet. With a sweat. He pants. The People chant him comfort. They begin to bear him home. Nonosabasut, by himself, by himself, watches them labour up the cliff-face.

On the birch, a bright red stain . . . .

The Micmac party don't know this speaking part of the People's river. Wearing whiteman's hats and whiteman's shirts, they beach their canoes and scout the rapids' edges, eyes on shifting waters, gauging the crowd of rockheads. It is said by the People that the rocks are giant frogs, once turned to stone, before the coming of the smaller frogs with the whitemen. The Micmacs haven't left their guns in their nailed canoes. Their canoes are rounded on their bottoms like a whiteman's boat. They know they are by one of the People's rivers.

Their leader's shadow lies still across a slide of water as he stands where he has leapt upon a boulder. He points a way through the foaming maze for his party to follow.

Watching, from the other side, the People cannot hear the sound of their strange talking because of the speaking river. The People could easily kill most of them. But Nonosabasut decides. Leave them. They are going downriver to the whitemen, not threatening the People. Without speaking the others decide this too. Wothamisit is sick. There are two children unable to walk, as well as the old woman Oolanake. Their trek homeward upriver will be slow because of that. Fighting will only delay it more. And what if the caribou come early and the other People can't manage by themselves and it is again every man for himself as it was that time with Osnahanut's grandfather? They watch.

The Micmacs have two canoes. The first, with the leader, begins the run the same way the People do, but then the snarl of water on the large rockface where the left channel starts frightens them. At a shout they slap water, charge and bounce along a narrow rocking passage into where the water seems to rest. But that is a bad place. It is a place where many thrusts of water wrestle with each other, locked and motionless. As when hot stones are flung into large birchbark kettles and the water starts its boil with slow seething. And when their boat strikes this pool, hands grapple, it spins sideways, tips, is wrenched round again. THROUGH! THROUGH! Paddles making celebration in the air.

The leader stands and gestures a warning for the second boat with his paddle. But already this canoe is aiming, bodies crouched, knees locked sensing eddies. They don't see him and they follow blind, bounce through the chute ... HAIOOO! HAIOO! But the pool dashes them next second with open boastful mouths, arms spread, into the wrestling waters. Three grab the gunwale and tackle the snakeback river with their boat, fighting it at last, to shore. But one man cannot grasp it. He gets beaten on the frogback rocks and comes out bloody, thrashing, sinking. The leader in his canoe watches him. He will surely snag him coming down. But as he comes he makes no motion. The man is in clear water now. Their chief's canoe could reach him easily. Is it an enemy he wants to die?

The Micmac goes under another time. The shore is far. His head is bloody. He is floating, hair wild, thrashing weakly. Disappears another time. His head again! But no one moves to help him. Under again. He hits the gravel-bar but, no strength to stand, he rolls right over it.

He is a log now in the shallower water. Limp and rolling, hands without feeling for the stones they slide across.

When he is beached his party goes to him. They lean over him. But it's no use. He is dead. They show great grief. The chief especially. He rips a small necklace from himself and lays it on the body. He kneels and grinds his hair with mud. Then they carry the deadman over the crumbling red earth embankment into the bush to bury him.

Osnahanut says —Wothamisit has told me of this. These strange people let their own men in danger die, even when it is possible to save them. They say it is too great a debt to owe your life to another man.

Nonosabasut stands. He notches one of his special decorated arrows, pulls the tall bow back hard and lets fly. Quicker than a bird it flashes over the People's river and beds itself between their two canoes on the far shore at the spot where the Micmacs have mourned their drowned brother.

Safe, on three sides water, Longnon's People have been
living on this long peninsula, this thin bone of land
where the brook joins the widest part of the People's
river, living here through the spring and summer in the
last few years, able to manage without going to the seacoast and the islands by making spring kills of caribou
returning from their winter feeding grounds. As they
beach Nonosabasut's party see Longnon's People have
already left to travel up to the great lake to help with the
deerfences there. There are fifteen winter-style mamateeks, six-sided, firm low earth walls bearing cone roofs.
They preside over the wide big river's shoreline, well-
hidden just behind a thin line of birch, spruce and alder.
Behind the mamateeks is a swath of forest then the
peninsula's other shore, a long shore, straight, where the
smaller river's current, slow by now, runs along its
length to join the main river at an easy angle.

Two years ago a smaller group with Demasduit's and
Osnahanut's widowed mother, by then remarried and
with other children, tried a similar settlement on islands
near the south shore, but one night furriers surprised
them, surrounded their mamateek. The snow still lay
crusty but hollowed underneath. The group fled, at first
together, then separately. The woman running last,
without her racquets, had fallen through the weakened
snowcrust and the furriers had caught her, knifing her
through the chest as she knelt with her robe drawn
open to show she was a woman. That gave time for
the others to reach their canoes. They returned safely
later to find the old woman and carry her to the shore

where he, Nonosabasut, and her son Osnahanut saw her a few days later in the spring sunshine, the snow over those few warm days by now yellow and almost melted.

The People make a fire inside one mamateek while they unload canoes in the drizzle. Two canoes they carry across the neck of the peninsula to the small brookside for emergency escape.

When Nonosabasut laughs he feels most alive and they are all laughing remembering their joke of taking the boat. Then they tell their other tales. Last year, in early spring, the whitemen climbed up out of their deep sawpit, a large pine still resting in it, not cut through yet, their hair plastered with snow and sawdust, in an absolute fury because it was the third time they'd had snow shovelled down on them, slushing down their hot necks, making it even muckier at the pit base, breaking their two-man saw rhythm so their arms would stiffen and they would almost fall off their platforms into the deep sawdust well below them. And since they were being paid by the log sawn, it was no laughing matter.

Nonosabasut had often watched how the foreman came at the end of day and counted the logs sawn, then handed the men those metal pieces. What kind of men were these to sweat in a deep pit all day with that hard sound in their ears and only a cavemouth of sky to look up at?

But that was all last year. This year Osnahanut and he had thought of a better trick still. Coming across the stretch between the two needle-islands they had seen whitemen stalking a fine goose from their boat in a narrow cove. A man stood in the bow with his gun pointed.

The whitemen were not careful enough and the goose flew off from them across the headland, but they continued in search for it. Later, in the evening, he and Osnahanut had taken the small canoe and captured this same goose. A really huge one. When Demasduit had skinned it, Osnahanut stuffed it with moss and some twigs, and Shawnadithit, his young niece, had sewn it with fine treeroot, carefully puncturing the downed skin with her tiniest sharp awl for the holes.

Hidden next day where they knew the same men would pass, Nonosabasut and Osnahanut left the goose, floating on a long line. The men chased it, one rowing, the other pointing his musket. Up close they fired. The shot breached the water but the goose did not stir. As they came closer Osnahanut pulled the line in. Again the man fired. Again the goose floated. Up to the beach Osnahanut pulled it. The men leapt from their boat, leaving their muskets. He and Osnahanut leapt up, arrows notched ready. Slipping and scrambling the men fled back to their boat, and lay behind it, soaked, as they let fly their arrows. Keeping behind it as a barrier, the men swam it out of arrow-range, terrified, one of them half drowning pushing the rudder. . . .

Warm morning. Peace for a moment as he wakes. One lightshaft through the smokehole brightens the ash-white hearth. Black skeletons of forked sticks left undestroyed by the fire shine in the morning light. If he touches them they'll crumble like old bones.

He and Demasduit, on the ledge away from the hearth by the sloping bark wall, are in darkness. The sun, inspecting everywhere, hasn't found them. He is warm as if it is full summer and he is lying in an open place where the sun can touch him. But he and Demasduit are in their own warm darkness.

Part of the warmth is her legs lying clasped with his, her legs apart, his own thigh between them, the special warmth there where her body begins. His hand feels where her breasts are full again. Their sleep-robe smells of her sweet milk, of their two bodies, of fur and of the fresh spruceboughs he brought in last night for the sleeping hollow.

Ever since he was a child, waking in a mamateek, he has felt safe and free. His People are here now, ALIVE now. And why not tomorrow, the next day? A change is coming. But he'll persuade them how to meet it. Wothamisit is right. They should keep away from the whitemen until they grow stronger, and not tempt them.

No more rain. It's a clear day.

Without waking Demasduit he sits. He counts those of the People who will spend winter together in the big mamateek when they reach the People's lake. Sixteen. He gazes at the four other couples in their own sleeping hollows. On the ledge this side are five children cuddled

32

together. Shawnadithit's mother, Doodebewshet the old butcher, is bent like a bow herself on the other side. And then there is himself and Demasduit. The sun is shifting slowly towards Osnahanut's face. He'll wake soon. Over Demasduit, a spider swings on a long thread, catches himself and begins his tracery.

The walls are hung neat—clothes and parcels, birchstrips still not sewn, three hides, two beaver pelts, a stone axe, a metal axe, ironheaded spears, bows and quivered arrows. His own bag is by him. It holds the two hemispheres of his father's that the People use for starting fires. On the floor are the things the People took out of the boat's cuddies: many pots and metal kettles, some clothes with clever buttons, even a trap. Over it all, tying it in two bundles, the sails.

Insects amble up the sunshaft—a bright wasp, spinning flies, feathery mosquitoes. Quiet. With great peace of heart he goes outside. Perhaps Wothamisit and the others will recover. On such a day there could be no dying. A mist still holds the river but the sky is fresh and almost clear. A low sun signals red between the trees. His footsteps scatter mice. By the shore he bends to cup still water. Over his eyes. Another handful in his mouth. A drop from his chin blurs his image in the water. Bright green pebble by his hand. Smooth it lends itself to rubbing with his thumb. His nail can scratch it. He keeps it. His knees are awkward on blunt stones. He stands and breathes. It would be good to spend another night here—his favourite place. And if they were lucky, a last salmon run might be travelling up the smaller river and they could catch it in the shallows at the peninsula's end. Already because the mist has thinned he can see another stretch of beach along the river. Soon a wind touches him. Mist stirs. Morning's light turns golden.

Suddenly he can see the far shore. SMOKE!

He turns, he runs. The People are awake. He shouts —No fires! Smoke across the river!

The People begin to gather everything . . . .

Warm weather, easy travelling, no smoke for three days, to the People's lake is only a day's canoeing. Barefoot Nonosabasut straddles two frogback boulders. He hears the riverrun. *I stretch long arms into salt ocean bringing this good fortune.* Beside him, behind him, in front of him, like trees in the river's mouth the People stand facing downriver.

The two children have recovered, and old Wothamisit is able to sit in the sunshine watching the People make this living fence across the brookmouth.

The salmon run's scouting edge has gone by. The People await the main dash. These late ones must have escaped the whiteman's nets when a moonlit tide poured them wriggling into funnels of rivers.

The stream tugs at the points of his forked spear. On the bottom are small stones. He plunges at each within his spear's reach. To guard its children the river, as all waters do, deceives a man's eyes and deflects his aim. He tests its cunning. Any moment now the salmon will appear. As he stares into the rush between his widespread legs it seems as though the water has become still, and he, a giant huntgod, is flying swiftly over its iron surface.

Then Osnahanut shouts. The water swarms. He leans and stabs. A spurt leaps past his thrusts, like a hurled silver spear. And then a quiverful hurtle chest-high past him. Thrust and thrust. Everywhere across the rapids, dealing death, the silent People's forks are pinning the salmon's deft rushes. He snags two large ones. Their struggles unbalance him as he wades and flings them shorewards, gasping in the drowning air. He falls into bloody waters in the crowded river. Tails still thrusting his two fish vault up the bank into sprucetrees. As he flounders a salmon-pelt bruises him. Thrust and thrust. Just one this time. Everyone is stumbling in the cluttered water. Careful, careful.

On the bank is Waunathoake, excited, screaming by a thrashing pile, running after those that blind-vault back to water. Red. The shallow brookmouth reddens. Demasduit is yelling to him —Husband, help me!

Somehow she is clutching three, afraid to walk in case she falls. He grabs tails and hurls with all his strength. They land by Wothamisit who is clapping and laughing as the People whoop and fall. Get better, Wothamisit. Good food, warmth, this winter we must hear your stories, last of the old men, who else to turn to? And the coughdeath won't become you, Wothamisit, much-loved old one. See the silver riverfish are dancing for you, old one, wise one . . . .

It's over. The People face upriver where the salmon-run, in deeper water now, from bank to bank proceeds, its passing like a squall-cloud's driven rain, in sudden thunder . . . .

With the large salmon catch, the goods from the whiteman's boat, and Wothamisit to carry, it is a hard push upstream. Further up, there is a stronger current yet, where the last bend breaks the lake's emptying force into wild rapids. There are quieter waters by the east bank but the People will still be too tired. Nonosabasut will call a stop at a landing place and send word to the sandy point on the shore where Longnon's family should by now be settled.

But Longnon and his People are already at the landing-place.

—The People have been waiting for you, Nonosabasut, and this morning we decided to come here to see what help we might give if you came today.

Longnon is pleased with the salmon catch and the partridge. Demasduit gives him some egg-pudding because neither he nor his family have been to the bird-islands this year. The taste is a remembered pleasure to him.

Longnon's family has prospered by staying on the peninsula. He recounts the season's news of People in the other mamateeks, all now returned. There've been many skirmishes with Micmacs and a few with whitemen. A large canoe with Shendoreth's family, caught in a squall, was overturned, one whole mamateek drowned at once. And down the deerfence about two days' travel, a fire has gutted the valley. So there's repairing to do.

Some of the People travelled to build it up there but it was no use because some places were so barren they had no trees to break and no bushes to weave together.

—That's bad news, Longnon. What can we do about

37

it? We don't really have enough People to send any there to camp, and wait, and hope to scare the whole herd into the rest of the fence. Might have to, though. What about the lynx, have they left their den yet?

— No. Not yet. The caribou won't come for a few days. But you never know, Nonosabasut.

Nonosabasut comforts him —At least the fire in that valley will make easier hunting next year of other game.

It was always a dark place with very tall trees so that nothing would grow under them and in all the times he has travelled that valley there has been no living thing under the ancient trees or in them except dark-loving fungus and moss. Now there will be good browsing and birds will be singing in new bushes next summertime and different trees from before will spring up making it pleasant to walk there.

Wothamisit is sick, but he knows more about deer-fences than anyone. He'll tell the People what to do about the barren places.

Then Longnon and Nonosabasut make a reckoning of the People, Longnon drawing fine lines with a stick in the sand to show those winter mamateeks that are built new and those that are abandoned. With the drowning and old people dying and some of the very young children also, there are two fewer mamateeks this year than last year and some mamateeks have fewer people in them. Maybe before winter is over some of these with few in them will go in with others. With the stick Longnon marks each person inside each mamateek's circle.

Nonosabasut, his mind on the caribou, reckons how

many bowmen are needed in trees, how many at the first turn, and how many at the second where panic jumps on the caribou's backs and they stampede. There are really only fifteen who are agile, fast-bowed, and spear-handy enough to make a good show of the dangerous postings at the chute's end, where the animals, searching freedom, throw up their heads for a moment and so catch arrows in their throats if the bowmen have stood fast and are quick enough.

Shawnadithit tells them that this year she will join the group at the chute's end. Longnon is silent. In his father's time no women would kill at the fences, they would wait for the men to return to the sandy point with the carcasses, then do the labour of skinning and dressing while the men roasted haunches and rejoiced. But for years now women have helped at the first turns, thrusting spears and pounding arrows into fear-smelling brown skins so that the men at the fencemouth had an easier time of it. Longnon speaks —For that, Shawnadithit, you must have a good spear and a strong arm as well as a true arrow.

Osnahanut says —I'll make her a bloody good spear. There's that iron trap I found in the woods last year, the one with the forefoot caught in it. The lynx had bitten right through to escape. I'll make her a strong broad point from that. You just watch the caribou she'll bring down.

—So much for the good spear. No doubt, Osnahanut, you will give her a strong arm and a true arrow as well, if you haven't already!

Osnahanut is angry, but Longnon smiles in his eyes.

—Don't mind me, Osnahanut. I'm an ageing man with no courage who doesn't dare to venture down our river to the islands. Don't take notice of me. There've been so many changes. An old man can't keep up with them. Who is to say that Osnahanut, who is in every way a full man, and Shawnadithit, in every way a full woman, should not live together and bear children? And in these hard times every hand that can help is valuable, though I hate to see old customs trampled like spring snow on well-used paths. . . . Ah, sons and daughters, I've missed the hard bounce of a canoe on saltwater and the scrape of shingle as we pull up on fresh beaches. This summer it was almost more than I could stand to recall the long journeys we made to the bird-islands. Nonosabasut, there was one of your father's great skills. Not only was he, like you, a man of song and wit, but also a man who could listen to skies and waves better than anyone. And it was his direction we followed in fogs to the great bird-island, even in total darkness because his knees could sense waves and currents so he knew how it should feel when we were right and how it would feel when we were wrong. Of course, he wasn't so much a forest hunter as my own father, his elder brother, and not so clever in judgement as you are, my young cousin Nonosabasut, but he was the last of the seers into the darkness, many counted him a shaman. No ceremonies for him though! A bit of a scoffer if the truth be told!

—Longnon. As my father knew how it should feel

when the direction was right and when the direction was wrong, so I feel to do what you do, to stay from the rivermouth and the islands in summer is the right direction for our People. You have pointed the way for us, you and your family. It's not a matter of courage, but a matter of wisdom. I will ask Wothamisit about those fences once we get to the sandy point. We should let him sleep as much as possible and not disturb him now. His soul may be talking with the gods, asking for help to recover.

Prow knifed into shingle, its dense boulder-ballast, skull-smooth, steadying it there, Wothamisit's canoe cradles him. He sleep-rests on a thick moss-bed over the cobblestones, half buried in its greensmell, beaver-robe warming his chilled bones. A sundream searches out his stone-pale face. He lies stone lonely. Silver riverrun nudges silvery canoe, it slightly swings.

Then dead-weight of its sleeping cargo eases bow down deeper in the fine shingle and its stern again rests. So it is with old Wothamisit as day by day he eases further with the weight of age and sickness into his last long sleep. As a man sleeps each night his soul learns how to leave him, until the one day when it leaves him forever. So Wothamisit has taught the People. And that is why the word the People have for the short sleep of nighttime is the same as the word for the last long sleep. And that is why all those things that have no life are said to be sleeping.

Shivers from the trembling river stir Wothamisit's sewn birch bed. They pass through him. They pass through the People watching where he lies. In the changing forests behind them, more birchleaves than there are bright stars fall and fall and fall.

Osnahanut has draped Wothamisit's tent with the sail as he has promised. Wothamisit, waking from many good sleeps, rises and goes to the entrance. Happy to be home by the great lake. And maybe the caribou feasts will recover him.

Demasduit, exploring with the others the pile of goods from the boat, has found a whiteman's chest covering. One of those armless coats which buttons down the front. She takes it to Wothamisit to wear under his robe because wrapping him close it might bring him comfort.

Wothamisit is pleased. The People gather around him. He says —I had many good sleeps. I dreamed about my sons and my grandson. Speaking with them has brought peace to me.

Shawnadithit brings him warm water. She puts the birchbark vessel into his shivering hands.

—Drink and rest well, Wothamisit. Now you're safe by the People's lake. A few good caribou feasts will recover you. We're looking forward to seeing you act out your stories of the old times again.

Osnahanut teases him —Well. What do you think now about going for that boat, eh? There. Not one lick of draught will bother Wothamisit in his mamateek this winter.

Nonosabasut asks him —Wothamisit, now the dark valley of the old tall trees where nothing lived has been burned down, how shall we repair the fence there? There's nothing to fell or weave in the usual way.

—Ah. I have an answer for you there, Nonosabasut. You remember I told you about the other deerfences there used to be when the People were many. There used to be one over there on that far side and three days down, over where the sun sets in summertime. I'm sure you've seen its remains. When I was a child, we went every year to a bare stretch of rock where nothing grew and how do you think we made a fence for the herds that used to travel that route? Well. It was clever I can tell you. We would plant thin poles wherever we could, at some places holding them up with piles of stones. Then we would tie on long strips of birch or cloth we had stolen from the whiteman's camps. Strange to say the movement of these strips in the slightest wind would be enough to make the caribou cautious. I have stood nearby, well-hidden, and watched a vast herd of them turn at the sight of these poles, even though there was good browsing just beyond them. There, I think, is your answer.

Coming from behind, in the dark mamateek, the coughdemon picks up Wothamisit and rattles him. Wothamisit struggles hard, gasping, and shakes him off. After his fight he leans back on Demasduit and Shawnadithit. They wipe bloody spittle from his cracked mouth. Osnahanut in watching silence drops a pebble from the campfire into a bowl of blueberry juice and brings it. Wothamisit sips its sweet warmth. He rubs his chest covered with the whiteman's chest-coat. The chest-coat has a smooth slippery lining. His sweat is making it sticky.

There are two slits in the front of it. It feels like a pebble in one of them. Wothamisit fingers it out of the small pocket.

Nonosabasut says —That is one of the whiteman's talismans. Maybe it is kept for luck like my father's quartz crystals. Many times I've seen whitemen take this thing out of their clothes and open it and look at it, as if wondering what to do. And then they would snap it shut and stop what they had been doing and go off and do something else. And once I saw a man shake it by his head and put his ear to it to listen to its spirit talking.

Wothamisit shakes it. He holds it to his ear.

— Listen. I can hear its heart beating.

They all take turns listening. Then Nonosabasut tries to open it.

He puts his fingernails in a thin crack around its edge trying to force it open. Then by accident he feels a place that gives when he presses. The talisman snaps open. He drops it. Now they can see a strange design with two tiny arrows pinned at the centre.

Osnahanut picks it up. There's another thin crack he gets his fingernails into. Snap the back comes off with his pull. In his hand the talisman is moving. Shiny as sunlight with red eyes gleaming, the talisman is moving and its heart beating inside its golden skin.

The People gaze at it. Then Wothamisit takes it in his hand.

— This is very fine and very beautiful, this spirit. I wonder what magic it does for the whiteman.

— It's your magic now, Wothamisit.

Wothamisit turns it in the sun, watching it glint, its red jewel eyes staring back at him. It beats like a tiny drum. He turns it again. Then it falls from his shaking fingers. He snatches for it. It drops against his knee and disappears.

The People jump up.

—In the blueberry juice! It fell in there!

Demasduit begins giggling at the memory of it. The red jewels, the bright clever metal, the serious beating of its heart. . . .

Osnahanut is afraid to put fingers in to search for it. He tips the juice out carefully. There it is. On the bottom. He picks it up. Its heart has stopped.

Demasduit's laughter like a sewing thread stitches round the group.

Osnahanut announces —It's drowned! It's drowned!

He dances. He rolls on the ground laughing.

Old Wothamisit, the joke's cause, can only allow himself one slight smile.

Nonosabasut has been singing, flames dancing to his voice, Osnahanut's hammering following his rhythm. Osnahanut has worked on the flat base of the iron trap but cannot make it take a deer-spear shape. He has made several arrowheads for the People for the hunt instead. They point a line beside him. Now he is beating at an axehead he found in a place where trees had been cut last summer. This axehead has been made by folding a single plate around to form a socket for a shaft. Then the two long ends of the plate have been beaten tight together to make a blade with one extending further than the other to make the cutting edge. Containing the fire's heat in a small oven of piled stones Osnahanut has been able to flatten the axehead back into its original width, just the right size for a broad spearhead for Shawnadithit. It glows red now as he pounds a heart shape and beats its edges thin with a hammer-stone. His father used a sharp deer-antler to chip the edges of stone arrowheads in the old days, its resiliency causing his blows to vibrate through the tip so that, like a voice echoing from cliff-sides, each blow was doubled or tripled. But the metal's heat makes it impossible to use antler as his father did. The times he had tried it, it charred and blunted. His father had been able to fashion points for spears or arrows in less time than it now takes him to build a small fire. But stone-tips are always chipping and cracking unless you are lucky enough to find a hard glassy kind not quite too hard to work with as some stones are. And iron you can always resharpen. Besides it's always difficult to chip good long shanks in stone so that the points will attach firmly to their wooden shafts. With iron that's no problem. Strangely his father had known all about iron. How fire was needed to soften it, stones of a certain shape to beat it on, and water to keep it tempered. His father's grandfather spoke of another time very long ago, long before the cruel ones, when the first tall ones from the sea had visited the northern coast and shown the People all these things. And the tradition had been passed down so that when the cruel ones came in large numbers the People already knew how to use the metal they brought with them and left rusting in the forests. Finished. He throws the shaped spearblade into water. It steams and spits.

—I'll grind its edge sharp tomorrow, Shawnadithit.

Shawnadithit is finishing a ceremonial robe for him. With a knife she is working on the thin bone pendants for the fringing. Once pendants were scratched lightly, but since her grandmother's time the People have been using iron knives to cut the lines sharp and deep. She copies some designs carefully from pendants on an old robe of Doodebewshet's. Every design on every pendant is different from every other, some diamond shaped, some triangular, some like ladders, some like trees. In the old days the meanings of the designs were known but they are now forgotten. These pendants are usually buried with a person when he dies. She makes them carefully.

—You're very hot, Osnahanut. Can I get you a drink?

—Yes. I think I'd like to walk out to the point. Coming?

Nonosabasut sees them leaving. What will the People

say if they build a baby together, they being so blood-close? Still. This has been going on for some time now and maybe no baby will ever come out of Shawnadithit. Wothamisit was telling him not so long ago that the women had more babies when he was young. Some now have none at all or ones that are weak. And there are no longer enough People to marry out of the family completely. *That is the trouble, Nonosabasut. See how these children are all looking so like each other. Much more so than you or Longnon. Even Demasduit was very unwell while building up Waunathoake. But now there is another you must build up together carefully.*

Demasduit is drowsed by the heat of Osnahanut's fire. Nonosabasut lies close beside her. Osnahanut and Shawnadithit will be by the lookout pine by now. Flooding the close woods like the searching waters that jam behind beaver dams in springtime, herds of caribou are slipping through the tumbled lowlands, lining up along ridgetops, their heads down, browsing on mosses, reeds, eel grass and lichens in buzzing swamps. They are silent under the watching moon. One day soon they will reach the People's lake and will be spotted from the pinetree on the end of the sandy point where Osnahanut and Shawnadithit are watching how still the lake is under the gazing moon.

He dozes too and dreams he is riding a huge stag, the herd leader. Then he is the stag. He is trying to lead his herd safely past the deerfences, but they won't follow him. He cannot speak. He can only nudge this one and that one with his heavy head . . . too many to keep on the right track . . . try to panic them, to make them run fast and blind . . . suddenly whoops and shouts . . . whitemen chasing them . . . guns spitting fire and bellowing in echoing valleys . . . run Demasduit . . . run Waunathoake . . . she can't run fast enough . . . Shawnadithit, Longnon, Osnahanut, Wothamisit, running running. . . .

Down down. No breath in him. Others are falling on him like stones. No escape, not even his head can lift. Darkness. Can't breathe can't breathe. . . .

He wakes. He's panting. He sits up. There is a man sitting by the fire. It's his dead father. His face glows in the firelight. His father reaches out and touches his neck gently. *Sleep, Nonosabasut. Bafu buth babashot* . . . .

Nonosabasut gets up. His father has gone. Demasduit is stirring because he is moving on their ledge. The fire, now his father has left, is dead also. He shivers. Cold. He lies up close to Demasduit again.

Shawnadithit and Osnahanut will be by the pine still, Shawnadithit feeling the bark against her back, Osnahanut heavy protection around her. Unused by children, her nipples are small buds. A wolf leaps. An owl descends. Death-screams skew out across the shimmering waters. Osnahanut empties himself inside her. His firm arms keep her from collapsing. Soon, separate, they will return. Under their feet the earth will feel new. And soon the moon will be gazing at other lakes and other woods.

*Bafu buth babashot.* His father was killed eighteen

years ago. The same year Shawnadithit was born to Doodebewshet. Perhaps he is sharing the fever Waunathoake had the day of the partridge hunt. There's a sweat on him and standing made him dizzy for a moment.

Eighteen years. There had only been the one canoe and Wothamisit had taken eight boys entrusted to him by their fathers. Crouched down behind the crumbling rocks of the shoreline the People kept back with their last arrows the advancing whitemen and their slaughtering muskets.

Rounding the point, Wothamisit guiding them through the needle-islands to hide their passing, he saw every beach littered with carcasses as he had seen it littered before with the skinned seals the whitemen had killed.

Like the sea and the rocks and the empty sky, at that time he felt nothing. He listened only to the dip of Wothamisit's paddle and the rush of water along the canoe's silver sides.

First snow. Good killing weather. Already high crags glaze. Leaves blown down, the pale woods seem thinned. The People gather, comfortable in new hide shoes and leggings, sheltered in their huddle of mamateeks. Shawnadithit with her spear stands tall. Longnon's boy runs from the woods and down the shore to join them. He's been out scouting.

—No. The lynx haven't come back. They left yesterday and haven't come back. The herds are coming for sure.

Last night wolves howled far away on the other side of the People's lake.

First snow. It muffles their voices. Good killing weather. Longnon's boy is eager. It's his first hunt as a grown man. Longnon sends him up to climb the lookout pine. Herd-scouts might come swimming across the channel. They can catch three or four that way. A good start before the rest come in several droves over the next three days.

Wothamisit sits at his threshold. His lips are blue.

Nonosabasut calls out —Well, well, Wothamisit, we'll soon be filling your belly with feasting. That cough-demon will burp right out of you.

—Make sure you keep the hunt in order, Nonosabasut. Don't be too eager for the stringers. Catch the main clump, the does, as they squeeze together. Longnon's father used to say *Wait till you hear their antlers clacking together*. Then you know they're thick enough to shoot and run.

—Don't worry, much-loved old one. It would be better

you were there to guide us in it, but we'll do our best.

—I hope you put those poles quite close together the way I told you. Longnon is a good judge. If there's trouble, listen to Longnon. And make sure you stand your ground at the chute's end, you others! If some of you break and step sideways you won't get the killing spread right across. That way there's never going to be much of a pile-up. The rest'll just vault right over and then you've had it.

Shawnadithit heels her spear.

—I won't be the one to falter. You can bet on that. Wait till you see how many I get.

Wothamisit makes a strained chuckle.

—Ah. There's my girl. Just as bloody and full of guts as that old butcher your mother.

—Ha! Someone had to do that dirty job. Slaughtering captives isn't exactly a man's work, eh? So you had to leave it to Doodebewshet! Cowards! Couldn't even look them in the face when you killed them. The poor bastards got it in the back running away. Do you think my mother liked cutting their heads off after that?

Osnahanut pulls at her.

—Come on. He's only making a joke. He's really proud of you. He's been telling all his visitors what a woman you are to help us out with cutting that boat loose. He's so proud of that sail keeping the draughts out.

She turns to speak to Wothamisit again. But he's crawling back into his warm mamateek. Shawnadithit's old mother is coming—scowling, muttering, chewing a strip of leather dangling from her mouth, in her hand her large stone butcher-knife.

Longnon's boy shouts from the treetop —Hey! Hey! There's one out there already. A beauty. See him go.

Longnon calls him down —Come on, then. Here's your chance. Who'll go with you?

—Osnahanut. Osnahanut, will you paddle and let me draw?

Osnahanut grins at the boy. It will be the boy's first kill. And the first of the season too!

—Alright. If you think you can hit him square. You'd better take more than those two arrows though.

—What! I won't miss, cousin. And they've got your iron tips on too.

Nonosabasut is uneasy.

—Wait. Are you sure the deergod means this? If he's a particularly fine one maybe we should let him go. After all, with Wothamisit unwell last night the ceremony didn't seem to me to go as it should. I didn't have a good feeling about it. I've been hoping for some sign. Maybe we should show our gratitude by letting this special one go by?

—Oh, come on, Nonosabasut. Let the boy shoot. It's obvious the god has sent it specially for him.

They wait. They can all see the stag now. His head is a floating bush. Grey sky, grey waters. His warm life bears his great crown calmly through thin swirls of snow over the chill lake.

Osnahanut says —This is the one we should feast on,

Nonosabasut. I'm sure it's sent on purpose. This is the one to cure Wothamisit.

Nonosabasut gestures his permission. Osnahanut and the boy cast off. The People watch.

Close by, the stag sees them. He turns back into deeper water, his nose now high, his crown tipped backwards, swimming faster. A wake follows him. Osnahanut and Longnon's boy make the canoe lift with their speed. Close again. This time the boy draws and shoots. A miss. Osnahanut makes a quick turn, paddles hard, SHOOT NOW! Feathers of the second arrow show above the water. Its point is at the jam of neck and shoulder.

Longnon yells —Turn him! Turn him!

The animal is heading straight for shore away from the People. The boy paddles again. The canoe skitters about in its own length. Now they are right up to the stag's shoulder. Its antlers knock the bow. The boy leans and snatches. He hangs on. The canoe skids in crazy waters over the animal's back. Osnahanut stops them tipping. He could reach his spear and finish it in the spine but he gives the boy his chance.

The boy thrusts his weight down on the large head. Its neck is weakened by the arrow. A red stream is in its wake. Its nose tilts forward. The stag breathes water, coughs, jerks, boy hangs on. More water. It coughs again. Harder.

The stag will soon reach shallows. The boy pushes harder. Ah. It sinks. Its whole head sinks. Bubbles. Its motion weakens, stills....

Filled with summer fat its carcass **floats just below the** water. They tow it in. The People pull its hind legs up the bank. They're happy, shouting. Shawnadithit's mother bloods it with her mighty old stone knife. Nonosabasut stands there silent. Remembering his dream . . . .

The herd splashes downriver. Fences hem them to the water. Some thrash across the stream to try the other bank. The bank crumbles. Pebbles cascade. Another fence. No escape.

Then there's a break and they clamber through it thickly, following a leading stag. They snort into an alley through the woods. A good clear run. Noses point south once more.

The People watch them come. A large herd. Usually the largest follows on the second day.

Those in trees are waiting to promote a panic. They see this brown tide undulate, antlers reaching up like drowning hands. Step down on them. Paddle rapids of their passing. At the end stands Nonosabasut. Beside him Osnahanut. Shawnadithit. Longnon. Longnon's boy. The others from the far-shore families. They see while crouching how the alley fills. Tight, neat, each swinging belly. Perfect packages to slit. The earth will reek with blood and offal. Sever each limb. Still this ceaseless motion. Arrows notched, their perfect feathers slide between worn fingers. Nonosabasut whispers the bow song.

> Don't fail string
> Shaft fly true
> As bird flew
> As shaft grew
> As clear morning
> As spring certain
> No time more to sing
> The singing was well done before.

His voice is lost in thunder. Their spreads tangle CLACK CLACK as they jostle. Close arrows bury feather deep in hollow ribs. Five drop at once. Others leap them. Full stampede. At the chute's end they lift heads, THWOCK THWOCK, catch arrows in their throats crash down legs snap eyes craze. Other stone-sharp hooves pound out their last breaths.

Winging his full quiver it appears to Nonosabasut as if the pile, like one body, comes rolling nearer nearer, as each throat shows until, too close, he reaches for his spear and catches the next brown leap-up in its chest. It knocks him and he tumbles too.

Voices call to him. He lies alone. He rises dizzy. Three other frantic bodies vault his way. He drops again. They pass over him. He rolls. He crawls. He runs. The herd's last beasts are falling down like rain. They scramble, run, crash free. A moaning silence. And by now the People from the trees and chute's first bend come hunting quiverings in the mound. With spongy thrusts of spears, they still them, blood now from the pile in the low spots like red rain.

They start to drag the bodies to the shore.

Shawnadithit's mother supervises skinning, cleaning, quartering. All day they labour.

Men transport the meat to the sandy point. They lay it in heavy piles. They dance on it to press it down, then cache it in the storehouses, loading rocks on top.

All neat again.

Another herd tomorrow. Maybe two. Not too cold to

chill your fingers. Not too warm to rot your prize.... It's good killing weather.

But no deer come.

Since the wind has changed the People think it is the smell of death. The second day they clear the chute's end. They dig a special hole and ceremonially grind each bone to powder. The powder blocks noses. They sneeze. Its ash-taste clogs their throats. They tip the powder in the hole and cover it. But no deer come.

Next day Osnahanut whispers to Nonosabasut that maybe Wothamisit's poles aren't working in the burned valley. Maybe the first herd was a lucky gift. What bothers Nonosabasut is that the wolves still howl from far away and the lynx have not yet returned. Perhaps Osnahanut is right. Perhaps the herd is turned another way.

—We'll travel fast. Just you and me, Osnahanut. We'll follow the fence down and see what's happening.

They take their gear. They take a small canoe.

They find the poles are undisturbed. And there are no herd-tracks crossing there either. During that night they mark the direction of the wolf-howls. Next morning they go west. They cross the high points of three streams. They come across the remains of old deerfences. These are the ones Wothamisit has often spoken of.

In one clearing they sight a caribou. A sick one. It is lying down. Hearing them it rises. Panic drives it. Jogging, they can follow it. They let it make some distance knowing it will bed again. They walk but do not stop.

In two hours they have reached another ancient fence. Despite the new growth everywhere its outline is clear to see. Trees are cut through the trunk higher than a man stands until their tops can be pushed over to fall against the next tree which is cut the same height, felled and its fallen branches woven in the gaps. The caribou has tracked the clear course. When its print looks fresh they move more cautiously.

Then they hear a snort and crash in front of them.

In a clearspace the sick caribou has been hemmed in by a lynx pair. Nonosabasut recognizes the pair from their set. The female with her dragging belly. The male with his hind quarter mangled in some struggle years before. Usually they hunt the stragglers at the beginnings of the People's deerrun but they have come this far searching as Nonosabasut and Osnahanut have done.

Now Nonosabasut knows where the deer have gone to. They have changed their route for some reason, to the west end of the lake where the huge herds used to go when both the caribou and the People were many. Maybe the killing in the east route has been too regular. Perhaps that small herd was all that the god could send the People this year.

He and Osnahanut watch the lynx pair. A leap. The male between its horns. Hind legs scratch soft mirrors from its eyes.

It stumbles blind. The snaking female charges. She rips its belly, claws along its neck, bites jugular. Frantic it lunges blind at trees, rolls, heaves onto knees, collapses, sighs. Each lynx snarls in, tearing for the steaming liver....

The storehouse has one-third its usual stock. The People make a trip to the western end of the lake, almost two days' journey. Nonosabasut leads parties every morning. They roam days for herds, try driving them down to shore, but without fences most stampede away. It stays good killing weather. But the People will live hard this winter.

They decide to spread the groups of mamateeks further apart. One group wants to remain at the western end of the lake. It will make each family's hunting space less crowded. Together the People raise mamateeks for this group on old foundations. Maybe the caribou will return that way in spring. There are two caribou feasts as is the custom.

One morning Wothamisit turns. He shouts. His People fill the mirrors of his eyes. They hold his hands. He dies.

*March 1819*

Nonosabasut sits with eyes wide but asleep inside himself. His eyes are filled with snow. At first it was voices. Whispers that trees made to him, snatches of songs, the sky singing, dead soft martens he'd unsnared and laid down on crisp snow speaking from behind him. Now it has become things he sees as well. For months he has been waking with a great peace inside him. He wakes up ten years old, the world new, hills to toboggan. Then Demasduit next to him, Waunathoake coughing in her corner, rouses him. (Nonosabasut? Who is *he*?) All day after his sweet morning dreams his mouth stays bitter. Not only with hunger.

Wood for fire. Snow for water. Move only when you have to. Each man keeps a small storehouse inside him.

Now it's a moon-cycle or more before the caribou return. During the moon's last growing, cold had bitten its way into the hearts of many. No news from the western People down the lake. When the caribou come back they will come back singly as always. Cows, calf-heavy, brooding, asleep, as the People are asleep and brooding. As the People are alone inside themselves. The caribou gather and gather. They crowd the white plain he stares at. Demons also gather in the birch around the plain. They make a deafening rattle. The caribou fall. They collapse, each in his own heavy roll of death. He can stop this if he tries.

But instead he becomes snow they die on. They press him. He becomes birch that demons shake, shake. Wind scatters him. Sun strews him about.

No-nos-a-ba-sut! No-nos-a-ba-sut! Someone is throwing
his name like counters in a knuckle-game. They fall.
Each one is etched with totems of the People's past. His
name rains down on him. He picks its syllables up. He
gathers them together. They become blank in his fingers.

—Nonosabasut!

Awake. Awake again. It's Osnahanut calling him.

He rises. His shadow has grown very long. What now?
The world is blank. What can possibly have stirred
Osnahanut?

—Demasduit. Her bleeding's started again. She's cold
and frightened.

Osnahanut himself is shivering. His eyes too are frightened. Nonosabasut rips bark off with his knife. That was
the reason he came to this tree several hours ago. On the
way back they chew the inner bark.

They have packed Demasduit with moss taken from
the mamateek's inner lining. The fire low. The mamateek's People listless. Nonosabasut's long rest by the tree
and the bark-juice have given him energy. He doesn't
take off his racquets. Instead he goes straight to her. She
doesn't speak. Turns her head against his hand. He takes
his bow from where it hangs. He takes a small wood
figure, one of the few things left behind by his dead
father. He takes a fresh caribou shoulder-blade. He
throws it in the fire. It cracks. He pulls it out. He stares
at it. Maybe the figure will give him help. In the bone's
cracks he begins to see the familiar lines of rivers and
the lie of forests around the great lake. He chants to the
figure. Then he stares again at the bone. Now a picture

comes to him. Caribou begin moving up the second river, strung out, forced into a herd by the narrow gorge there....

He stands. He makes commands. Wood. Water. Scrape this inner bark clean. Drive with this harpoon through the thin ice where the lake empties.

—Shawnadithit, sit for fish there. No need to go to sleep inside yourselves. Osnahanut and I will bring you meat in less than two days. The god has shown me.

They hack out the toboggan, load it with sleep-robes, their spears and bows and knives, and also a piece of sail to give them covering.

Already the People are stirring themselves. One goes to Longnon's People close by to stir them also. Nonosabasut holds hard to Demasduit and hard to Waunathoake.

—Well, Demasduit. Next year there'll be time to build another baby. You'll see.

Shawnadithit has been tending Waunathoake who stares at him with empty eyes. Shawnadithit's mother grumbles —Alright fools, get going, get going. You'd better come back with something for my knife or I'll be using it on you two for the stewpot.

As they pass, Longnon leans out from his threshold. He has bowel pains that jerk his face but he smiles and says —Go well, you two. Go well. My boy and I are off to hunt mussels and shellfish at the northern bay. We'll be back about the same time. If there're breaks in the sea-ice there we might be lucky. No use sitting here dying. They say you had a clear picture, Nonosabasut. Well. If the caribou are there we'll know now you are a shaman on top of everything.

Before night comes they stop by the swamp until the moon rises. Their feet crack off cattail tops. Sometimes, under the snow, there's grass still green. They search for it and find some. The green is sweet in their bitter mouths. Where the stream runs narrow the ice is thin and they hack out cattails from the frozen mud and chew their roots. In the quiet by the swamp as the light fails they hear reeds rustling. Osnahanut creeps along the far side, then walks into the reeds. Nonosabasut waits with his club ready. Suddenly muskrats dart towards him away from Osnahanut's terrifying feet.

Their legs make puffs in snow. He hits. He scrambles. He hits again.

He holds a crushed one by its tail and laughs.

— Here's a feast, eh Osnahanut?

Except for its toothy head and skin they eat it whole and raw.

Dark by now, and a chill afflicts them. They put on mittens and fur-lined robes, take off their racquets, and rest on the toboggan. From the swamp westward few trees grow. It will be easy travelling before the next valley crammed with trees.

The best way to get the caribou meat out would be straight down the river and back across the lake. A long haul compared to this approach. But they'd be stronger with good meals in them and could jog the whole day on the flat lake.

The moon rises. They are glad to walk again. They share the toboggan pull. Out of the trees in the barespace a wind catches them. Their right sides take the brunt. The night cold causes the snow to begin squeaking loudly. The toboggan bounces over snowbanks scarred by wind-claws like mud-flats after flood-time. The sky begins to place its stars. Ahead is a loom of woods they lean towards.

In the woods their faces unfreeze. They strap the toboggan tight, ready to carry it between them on its edge. But Osnahanut starts a hunger trembling. Nonosabasut has a headache himself. They sit to let it pass.

— Nonosabasut. If the god has sent us to the wrong place we won't even be meat for the People's stewpot. Hear that wolf-howl?

Osnahanut's jaw muscles tighten in a cramp and he pauses. He buries his head in his robe and waits out the painspell.

Nonosabasut decides — I'll go myself to make the killing, Osnahanut. And leave the toboggan here with you. If the deer come and I kill, all's well. I'll bring food back for you, brother, then we'll take the toboggan in and get the load out together. If the god means to fool me, and I don't kill, there's a chance you can make it back yourself from here with the strength you have left.

Osnahanut can't move his clamped mouth to reply. When he manages to speak he's not sure whether he's said anything or whether, as in a dream, he's imagined it. He wants to stand up, but can't rise. What's that roaring in his ears? A tremendous pressure shocks his stomach. It grows, then all at once gives. The noise leaves his ears. Smell of vomit. Then he notices it yellow on the snow. Nonosabasut is holding his head. The leather of his marriage-brother's coat smells, the fur trimming is a comfort to him as he leans on Nonosabasut, exhausted, but the world coming clearer.

— Don't worry. I'll go with you all the way, Nonosabasut. Be better in a minute. Wait.

They both stare into the dark woods. Just across this stretch of trees, and the caribou will be there. For certain they'll be there. If they're not there they'll have to wait for them. Always a little left, always a tiny spark to blow into flame a last time. They imagine the gully and the caribou padding on the snow, on the flat river-ice, and their lifesparks begin catching inside them.

They push on. . . .

They scramble down the bank of the first river. Only half as far as they have come left to go. But the moon is passing them by and dark catches up to them almost completely at the far bank. Along the flat river they make out hare tracks. They follow them in failing light to where they lead over the bank into trees. They set three snares. Dizzy and shaking they arrange the sail in the trees, lie close on the toboggan, and pile themselves with robes. Shivering stops, but pains and cramps keep them awake.

A morning hint of light comes through the sail. Osnahanut dozes. Nonosabasut lies there, his imagination reeling in and out of the long-ago mamateek, his People waiting, Demasduit and Waunathoake ill. Then he hears a baby's cry. He listens. He hears it again. Nonosabasut buries his ears deeper. This is the worst of the last few weeks. He would rather have Osnahanut's vomiting than hear these voices. The crying continues.

Suddenly Nonosabasut's headache seems to explode like a firelog. He hears a strong wailing over the baby's crying as if from a distance. But the wailing is coming from his own mouth. Sobs like a child's make his whole chest heave. Still the baby's crying needles his ears.

Osnahanut is leaping up beside him. Nonosabasut looks at him through his tears. Osnahanut is scrambling out of the sail-tent. He listens. The sail-tent is empty. The baby's crying turns to a scream then stops. Nonosabasut blinks and looks. Osnahanut is back again, leaning into the tent. Osnahanut smiles. He's holding a dead hare. The snare still dangles from its fur. . . .

So far Osnahanut has not vomited. They stewed the hare carefully, throwing stones from their fire into a birchbark bowl of melted snow until the liquid boiled and the meat turned grey.

The day is bright. The woods begin dripping as they go. Nonosabasut's lips move as if to sing, but he's too tired to make words jump to his tongue though he half thinks them.

They reach the height of land almost without noticing. The trees thin out, they make good time putting the toboggan down and dragging it over open spaces. Then the woods thicken again. The second river isn't far. Thicker, thicker, the toboggan becomes awkward to manage. . . .

They stare down on the silent river. It runs a deep trench, eroding banks cluttered with fallen birch. Because wind funnels here, its ice is almost free of snow. It glints blue in places, by its banks the surface is mottled like old skin. They can see a long way up, a long way down. Silence. And on the surface no motion except those slow whirlpools, those ghosts of running water that wind makes in the careless litter of snow.

— Will they come, Nonosabasut?

The toboggan rests aslant between two trees. Nonosabasut leans against a thick birch. The sun strikes his face. He breathes its gold air. Awake now, alive in this sun, the empty river stark white real, birch glinting like just-caught fish, every spruce sharp green, he wonders, is it here, away from the People, that Osnahanut and Nonosabasut will die, waiting for good luck to come out of a dream that was perhaps no shaman's dream, but a common one of his own making?

Down on the river their steps drum on hollow ice. As they walk fractures crack its metal skin like lightning. They hear its thunder. Skeletons of fallen trees sift full of snow like old boats beached. Their toboggan makes a neat line as they go. Across. Back. A short trek down the river's length. Looking. They still can't see. The bend is a mile or so. Turn round. The deer can't be downstream or there'd be some tracks here. . . .

—Either we hunt, Osnahanut. Or we sit and save our strength. What do you think?

—One hunts, one sits. One of us has to be strong enough tomorrow if they come.

—Alright, Osnahanut. Let me hunt.

—I'd argue with you, brother. But I know you've a better chance.

Just then Osnahanut vomits again. He rolls exhausted onto his back. He pants.

—Tell me, brother. Is the vomit red?

—No, Osnahanut. Don't worry. It's still yellow. I think you kept most of it down long enough that time.

Osnahanut watches a hawk. But the bright gleam of its wings hurts his eyes. He closes them. It would be so easy to let his body's life drain into the earth with the melting snow of springtime.

Nonosabasut's headache has come back. Perhaps that walking on the snow at night, and now today on the bright river, has bruised his eyes with too much shine.

He too watches as the metal hawk descends in its lazy spirals. It plummets. Marking with his eyes the place it falls he counts off trees to where the bank has stopped and left a bareplace.

—Alright, Osnahanut. Here I go.

In the trees' shadows there's relief. He lets his hair fall forward. Crossing the river he closes his eyes. He knows Osnahanut is watching him scramble up the bareplace. He counts the trees, pauses to line up his direction, and disappears. . . .

Nightfall, and Nonosabasut has nothing. They sit under a high pine's silence under a clouding sky. Osnahanut is afraid of a snowfall.

—I see it falling on us and burying us dead-asleep along with all the other asleep-dead things.

—That's a clever play of words. You can't be that far gone, Osnahanut, if you can come up with something like that.

—Well. I suppose we shouldn't grumble. We could always fill the toboggan up with these. What would the old butcher say to that!

On a flat stone plate over the fire, mud lumps are unfreezing. They begin twitching. Osnahanut picks one up. He frees a kicking frog. It has only one leg because Nonosabasut's hacking into the frozen mud at the swamp's edge has broken it off. As it kicks out of the mud, he throws each frog into boiling water. The frogs stew. When the water cools he throws another hot pebble in. It boils again.

—Don't worry, Osnahanut. I'm sure there'll be a beaver lodge up a creek I ran into a few miles down from here. That'll keep us going.

He'd hoped the hawk would be after martens or even hares. But it must have been other birdgame or a weasel he couldn't see. Not a thing to be found in those woods except a short line of foxprints over a crag. They didn't look recent either. It was an old high forest there, something like the place where the valley had burned. Not good hunting. He'd hacked the frogs out as a last resort.

—I think for your stomach's sake you should just eat

the legs, Osnahanut. I'll have the other parts.

— Alright. That stew-water goes down well. As long as there's something to be sick with it's not so bad.

They don't speak about caribou.

That night the snow falls. It colonizes every surface the sky looks down on. It covers the sail-tent as it covers the trees and as it covers every other dead or sleeping thing . . . .

Osnahanut wakes. Nonosabasut tells him —It's still snowing, but lightly, Osnahanut.

Nonosabasut's headache's better. They put on their racquets, pressing on loose new snow. Their coats hang from thin shoulders. When Osnahanut tries to smile his tightened face is like an ochred skull. His own hair has fallen out again during the night. Tying it back Nonosabasut's hands pull out more of it. The black strands disappear under the snow.

He skids down the bank, clinging as he goes. His racquets begin printing the clear river's surface like careful stencilling on a new ceremonial robe. He looks back at the record of his passing (light snow already blurring its edges), closes his eyes while he treads further, then opens them again to look upriver. Nothing. He squats. Because of the silence, the openness, he begins in a while to fall asleep inside himself. He's not surprised when far upriver he begins seeing caribou. They approach in a file. He hears a rattle begin in the birch-trees . . . .

He throws snow on his face. He slaps his face. They're

still coming! They're real! He waves up at Osnahanut. They're coming! They're coming!

He crosses the river completely. He hides there.

The file comes nearer, heads down and suffering. They draw close to the line his snowshoes have made. The lead cow crosses the line, the second crosses the line. Nonosabasut stands. The line stops. He approaches slowly.

The lead animal stands still and looks at him. She doesn't move. Muscles in her stricken legs are trembling. Her belly hangs almost to the snow. Her eyes are unblinking. Snowflakes dissolve as they land on her dark pupils. They melt there and spill. Her brown back is steaming. She looks at him. Unable to let fly he walks closer, until he stands near as a spear's thrust. The doe shivers. Something in her sack-belly tumbles. He's certain the swimming stag Longnon's boy drowned was the god's chosen deerfather. This is maybe the god's chosen deermother. There's only one thing he can do.

He lifts his spear—decides—and puts the flat of his blade on her rump.

— Go, mother. Go by.

She vaults clear in tremendous bounds up the fallen-down place of the riverbank into the woods.

But now the rest are alarmed. A long shot, but he lets fly at the closest. His spear pins a haunch but the deer keeps running. The spear drops out. Not deep enough. Blood pits snow like embers.

The caribou haven't seen Osnahanut. Nonosabasut runs hard to the opposite bank so the deer might continue their trek on the other side where Osnahanut waits.

But they all reach woods and stay in hiding. He retrieves his spear. He too hides. He can't see Osnahanut now for the snow. At least the wind is right. He waits. If they get back empty-handed after this . . . . The river's corridor blocks with snow. Fool. Why did he have to be so superstitious? He could have killed that one and maybe three others. Luck. Give luck, deergod, so that next year we can laugh and boast about it. Oh yes. Next year it'll be different. Don't go down to the sea at all. Get those deerfences built up. Get everybody together on them. They won't argue after the way things have gone this year. Then when the People are strong again they must make peace like the Micmacs have. Set traps and give furs to the whitemen for knives and axes. No more of this killing. He, Nonosabasut, would persuade them.

The snow keeps on falling and falling. A shout will carry no further than an arm's length. White moss fills the air. Crouching in thin woods he is becoming covered. Like any rock or dead fallen trunk. Somewhere nearby stand the caribou, sheltering against trees. Their warm backs allow the snow's delicate congregation now, their tired hearts fill with alarm as his fills with hope. Luck, deergod. Give luck....

CRACK. A gunshot! Again. It's from further downriver, the direction the caribou came from. Two more shots.

He listens in the white falling silence. Numbed under the tree's shelter he allows the snow to pile on his knees. Micmacs from the west coast must have crossed the watershed into the river defiles, expecting caribou to concentrate there. How many? Would they come down further? The caribou who escaped must have been at the front of the herd the Micmacs were stalking from behind. Fool. He could have had two of them easily. . . .

Nothing to be done about it in this storm. He becomes an empty cup the snow fills. Stiff from sitting, but he cannot rouse himself. Snow claims him as it claims the forest. It weighs on his shoulders as he waits, as he drowses. Let it own him completely. There's too much struggle . . . .

He leaps up. He shakes himself awake. Snow. Trying to smother him. No. He beats it all out of his hair, shakes it all off his coat so he can see the red stencilling. He's panting. Alive. The storm's passing. He jumps to the river. He yells —Osnahanut! Osnahanut!

An answer! He moves further onto the lake. Osnahanut looms towards him, stumbling through the thinning storm. They clasp each other. Osnahanut is collapsing. He holds him. Osnahanut has been downriver to investigate the shots. They were still butchering when he got there. But their toboggans were pointed homeward. No need to fear them. A large party, or he would have tried filching some meat under cover of the storm.

So Osnahanut was expending himself while he was sleeping in the woods. The shame brings a fire into his belly. Those caribou are still around the river. The squall is passing. Fresh snow, and he'll be able to trace them. He says —My brave brother. Build up the last fires in you. Our People are waiting.

As his courage-rage grows in him the snowsquall suddenly breaks. The river clears. Osnahanut is looking over his shoulder. Wordless he pulls Nonosabasut down into the snow. Then Nonosabasut sees them also.

Over by the steep part of the far bank, heads down in a line, are four caribou.

Bows from shoulders, arrows in their fingers. They edge closer. They each choose. Their arrows pierce feather deep. Two animals the god has sent them collapse slowly, their spreads like falling trees.

Their blood burns the snow....

Demasduit is growing stronger. Longnon and his boy arrived with mussels. The People held a feast and listened to stories of the caribou hunt, how the Micmac hunters had driven the herd in their way, how the god had sent the caribou after the storm because Nonosabasut had let the old mother go by.

Only Waunathoake stays ill. When he lifts her now Nonosabasut's arms remember the small weight of her when she was just born. She is almost as light again as she was then. His only child.

He saw her being born, allowed by the cluster of women to kneel by Demasduit's head where she could grasp his hands when her belly heaved. At the end she clutched his hair and pulled his face against hers as out into the light Waunathoake's dark head twisted onto the moss-pack, her tiny shoulder jerked itself free, and their whole slippery infant eased amazingly out of Demasduit's loosening belly. The cord still throbbed with life. Waunathoake cried out. Then the purple shadow on her skin disappeared as she drew breath, and dawn pink flushed over her. She was alive. He touched her. Her whole hand with its miniature fingernails gripped his finger. He laughed at the touch of her eager mouth but his finger was not what her blind mouth wanted. Demasduit took her to her nipple and they lay all together, three heads close and happy, the women murmuring endearments and soothing Demasduit's hurts. Even Shawnadithit's old mother humming to herself.

Their first child. Waunathoake mustn't die now. Just when the new baby they were building is lost. Spring is so soon. Yesterday Waunathoake drank good soup. All she needs is good food and warm sun. People don't always die with the cough. Children often recover. And she was so happy last summer, chuckling and leaping as seawaves foamed over her round belly. There's no belly there now. Last summer her belly had fitted into the cup of his one hand as he lifted her high and squealing over his head. A firm, tanned little ball she had been then.

He cuddles her close now, humming her asleep. Must keep her warm in the beaver-robe. Recently she'd stopped fretting. There was once a few months ago she'd kept bothering him as he sat shaping a spearshaft, and she threw away food Demasduit gave her in a fit of temper. He'd shaken her and she'd cried, and holding her, angry, he'd felt her fever and was sorry. Listening to her crying and saying—Waunathoake hurt, Dada pushed— he felt sick in his heart then and feels the same way now, remembering. Now her cries at night are soft whimpers. Her eyes contain no recognition of him. Her mouth is cracked and lifeless. How delicate and full were her lips last summer.

He sits and stares, trying to have a good dream about her. If he can recapture the feeling he had when the god spoke to him about the caribou. He tries remembering that feeling. But already it seems so long ago, and as if it had happened to someone else.

He's alone in the mamateek with Waunathoake. He stares at the walls hung neatly with the People's things. Every time Waunathoake whimpers or coughs he goes to her and holds his fingers by her face to make sure she keeps breathing. Every morning he wakes and immediately looks at her. Sometimes, waking early, in the dark he has a great fear inside him that he has slept while she has died.

He takes his father's bag down and pours out nine perfect quartz crystals. Their clear chiselled sides rest in his lined brown palm. If there were a shaman he could get from him a chant so he could reach the sungod himself and ask for Waunathoake to live.

He hums, clenching the crystals in his hands. He lets words come from his mouth at random, chanting. He begins to rock. He calls on many spirits, then he breathes deep and casts the crystals down before him.

Bears. The nine crystals become bears in his sight. They are whitebears who live in ice, and out of the icecrystals they are emerging onto melting snow, and, yellow-muzzled frightening they are charging him so close he smells their damp mats of fur, sees their traps of teeth, their red tongues, chill eyes, huge paws like rotten rafts of spring ice . . . .

—Quick! Whitemen! The ones we took the boat from!

Demasduit, mouth trembling, eyes shockwide. She sweeps up Waunathoake. Behind her, Longnon, Osnahanut. He too moves now, speaks.

—Where? Stay and fight them. How many?

Longnon answers —They surprised us from the lake. Travelled with no fires. They have guns.

A shot. Very close now. The People are fleeing.

Demasduit flees, holding Waunathoake. Nonosabasut clutches her. She struggles.

—No. Leave her here hidden under the sleep-robes. They won't stop here. They'll chase us.

Osnahanut can see the whitemen. He shouts —They come, they come. Hurry.

Nonosabasut takes the baby and hides her.

—Run. Run.

They are running. Another shot. Nonosabasut stops. There are not four of them, only three. Demasduit! He sees her just now coming from the mamateek carrying Waunathoake. She is screaming and crying, holding her out to him. Whitemen close behind. He runs back to Demasduit. She stumbles, drops Waunathoake into his arms.

— Run, Nonosabasut, run!

He runs, runs. The People are in the forest across from the point. He too runs across the ice holding his baby and following the tracks of Longnon and Osnahanut. Shawnadithit waits for him in the trees. She takes Waunathoake. He turns. He starts back across the lake. Demasduit has fallen. Out on the ice after her come the band of whitemen. They are wearing furs. They come kicking through the snow to her, nine of them, stumbling across the lake to Demasduit, furry, shambling, ugly, cruel, like woken bears . . . .

. . . Mr——— loosened his provision bag from his back and let it fall, threw away his gun and hatchet and set off at a speed that soon overtook the woman. One man and myself did the same, except our guns. The rest, picking up our things followed. On overtaking the woman, she instantly fell on her knees, and tearing open the cassock (a dress composed

of deer-skin bound with fur), showing her breasts to prove
she was a woman, and begged for mercy. In a few moments
we were by Mr———'s side....

Nonosabasut takes his bow from his shoulders, notches
an arrow, and runs towards Demasduit. Osnahanut and
Longnon run with him. Osnahanut is shouting to the
People in the woods —They've taken Demasduit!
They've taken Demasduit! Follow us! Follow us!

Now there is a crowd running towards the whitemen.
Dragging Demasduit with them the whitemen retreat
towards the woods. Then they stop, turn, guns ready. No
cover for the People on the open lake. If they decide to
fire . . . . Nonosabasut slows down and pulls at Osnahanut's arm to stop him.

—Stop. Maybe we can talk to them.

All the People gather together. Nonosabasut tells
them —Maybe the whitemen are frightened because we
seem to be so many. Maybe they think there are more
of us ready to ambush them. Maybe that's why they've
taken Demasduit with them, as a hostage. I will go to
speak to them by myself. I'll tell them how the People
want to make peace with the whitemen as the Micmacs
have done. I'll tell them how we shall be friends with
them and will share our lands with them in peace. One
of you bring me a fresh sprucebough as a token.

—I'll go with you, Nonosabasut.

—And I'll go with you and Longnon too, Nonosabasut.

... After a pause three of them laid down their bows, with which they were armed, and came within two hundred yards. We then presented our guns, intimating that not more than one would be allowed to approach. They retired and fetched their arms, when one, the ill fated husband of Mary March, our captive, advanced with a branch of a fir tree (spruce) in his hand. When about ten yards off he stopped and made a long oration. He spoke at least ten minutes; towards the last his gesture became very animated and his eye "shot fire." He concluded very mildly, and advancing, shook hands with many of the party—then he attempted to take his wife from us; being opposed in this he drew from beneath his cassock an axe, the whole of which was finely polished and brandished it over our heads. On two or three muskets being presented, he gave it up to Mr——— who then intimated that the woman must go with us, but that he might go also if he pleased, and that in the morning both should have their liberty. At the same time two of the men began to conduct her towards the houses. On this being done he became infuriated, and rushing towards her he strove to drag her from them; one of the men rushed forward and stabbed him in the back with a bayonet; turning round, at a blow he laid the fellow at his feet; the next instant he knocked down another and rushing on—like a child laid him on his back, and seizing his dirk from his belt brandished it over his head; the next instant it would have been buried in him had I not with both hands seized his arm; he shook me off in an instant, while I measured my length on the ice; Mr——— then drew a pistol from his girdle and fired. The poor wretch first staggered then fell on his face: while writhing in agonies, he seemed for a moment to stop; his muscles stiffened: slowly and gradually he raised himself from the ice, turned round, and with a wild gaze surveyed us all in a circle around him....

Now he has fallen. He hears Demasduit fighting and screaming his name. Demasduit. He can't wing his own voice over to her across this drowning snow. The shock passes. He can see again. His blood is pouring out of him. Stop it, or he will die soon. He cups it in his hands like riverwater. It flows into his hands. It overflows his hands onto the snow. Demasduit. Silent now. Her face is full of tears. He stares into the deep jar of her eyes. Nothing to say. Full circle. He, one of the last tall People, will die down and it will be these around him who will tread down the People's forests. Full circle. He is dizzy. He fixes each of the whitemen in his dying sight. Strange. A great calmness. Utter silence. Then suddenly he sees clearly . . . .

. . . his eyes flashing fire, yet with the glass of death upon them—they fixed on the individual who first stabbed him. Slowly he raised the hand that still grasped young ———'s dagger, till he raised it considerably above his head, when uttering a yell that made the woods echo, he rushed at him. The man fired as he advanced, and the noble Indian again fell on his face; a few moments struggle, and he lay a stiffened corpse on the icy surface of the limpid waters. . . .

# Demasduit

Demasduit sees smoke rise from his blood in the frozen air. Demasduit sees the snow burning. Her People hear her cries. They run onto the ice.

. . . While the scene which I have described was acting, and which occurred in almost less space than the description can be read, a number of Indians had advanced within a short distance and seeing the untimely fate of their chief haulted. Mr—— fired over their heads, and they immediately fled. . . .

No breath no blood no life. Nonosabasut is dead. He is dead on the People's frozen lake. Under the iron ice his soul is gliding down the river to the islands and to the churning sea where the sun rises.

A furrier brings a marked stick. Pulling Nonosabasut straight, he measures him. Careless he stamps on his black hair, bloody where it lies spread. Now his footprints too are red.

. . . For my part I could scarcely credit my senses, as I beheld the remains of the noble fellow stretched on the ice, crimsoned with his already frozen blood. One of the men then went to the shore for some fir tree boughs to cover the body, which measured as it lay, 6 feet, $7\frac{1}{2}$ inches. The fellow who first stabbed him wanted to strip off his cassock (a garment made of deer skin, lined with beaver and other skins, reaching to the knees), but met with so stern a rebuke from ———, that he instantly desisted, and slunk abashed away. . . .

Another furrier approaches in a bear crouch. He clutches at Nonosabasut's coat. She leaps at him. He cuffs her down. Then a young man with red hair grabs the furrier's collar. He pulls him by his hair and shakes him. The furrier ambles away, spitting and making a joke.

This young man is the one who caught up with her first, the one who first saw her breasts bared, who raised his hand against the others' guns. His cheekbones shine red in the cold out of his red beard.

The old man Nonosabasut caught by the throat sits still dizzy on the sled.

She looks behind her. Maybe the People will try crossing the lake further up by the gravel-bar to get behind the furriers. No sign of them anywhere. She's alone with Nonosabasut.

Waunathoake will be cold. But Shawnadithit will be holding onto her. Why didn't she listen to Nonosabasut? Why didn't she leave her under the skins in the warm mamateek? But they might have found her and roasted her on a stick, or taken her skin off and left her flesh lying there as they do with the animals they trap.

When the whitemen have left, the People will come back to the warm mamateeks. Maybe the whitemen will go soon so that Shawnadithit can give Waunathoake shelter. Will they kill her as they killed Nonosabasut before they leave? Maybe the red-haired man will stop them as he stopped them when he caught up to her and saw her bared breasts and raised his hand.

Now the deathshock begins its run through her opening veins like fever. Her tears pock the snow. Footprints, racquetprints, bloodprints. The blemished snow records his killing. Onto his face as she leans over him her tears splash softly. Her breath begins jerking.

Tearblind she hears a voice begin its wailing. The sorrows of her People through the ages. She listens to the ancient phrases, half-strange words. It's her own voice. Words fly from her across the snowplain into the shore's dark woods.

Where they go an eagle follows. It scouts the People's crags, lifts, then disappears.

... Both ——— and myself bitterly reproached the man who first stabbed the unfortunate native; for though he acted violently, still there was no necessity for the brutal act,—besides, the untaught Indian was only doing that which every man ought to do,—he came to rescue his wife from the hands of her captors, and nobly lost his life in his attempt to save her. ——— here declared that he would rather have defeated the object of his journey a hundred times than have sacrificed the life of one Indian. The fellow merely replied, "It was only an Indian," and he wished he had shot a hundred instead of one. The poor woman was now tied securely, we having, on consideration, deemed it for the best to take her with us, so that by kind treatment and civilization she might, in the course of time, be returned to her tribe, and be the means of effecting a lasting reconciliation between them and the settlers. ...

The old man on the sled beckons. They carry her and set her beside him. Her moccasin has pulled off. The young man who kept the furrier from taking Nonosabasut's coat, the red-haired man, bends down.

He ties her moccasin.

The sled moves. It leaves a straight track, precise as

etching on bone pendants. She keeps her eyes on Nonosabasut.

The lines of the runners grow closer and closer as she stares. The lines meet. Just afterwards Nonosabasut disappears. The snow, in cold evening now, continues to mark ... the wake ... of her own ... passing ....

Night of the second day. They mean to keep her.
But for what?
She had tried to help collect firewood but they wouldn't let her, waving their arms to say sit down sit down. The red-haired one gave her meat roasted on a stick, very hot. She scalded her lips.

She waits awake hours watching for her chance. Without snowshoes it will be difficult. But cold has come with a brittle sky and the crust might be firm enough to carry her if she treads carefully.

A man keeps watch at the spruce-shelter's end. They've placed her amongst themselves. She must step cautiously. Then she must push aside carefully one of the thin trees that make the shelter wall. The watchman's shoulders have slumped. A light breeze tousles his fur collar.

Moon bright.
Woods vivid.

This is the moment. She rises she steps her coat fringe grazes red hair she stops. One pace sideways balance.

She grips the pole. It won't move. Its branches are tangled with others. She bends, decided daring she heaves at its freshcut base, it shifts sideways. Enough.

She crawls through, continues crawling to the nearest

trees. Then she stands. She goes to move quickly, stumbles, the crust gives.

Shock still. Hands burn with cold. Listen . . . . Nothing. She pulls clear. She continues, slowly, holding onto branches to lighten her weight on the treacherous snow. When she falls the snow thuds into her breasts.

She stumbles all night, following the tracks. As she travels between them they open for her. They will lead her to Waunathoake. In Shawnadithit's arms, safe asleep in her warm mamateek, only maybe another hard day and night's journey. She won't stop. And how the People will greet her. And maybe even Nonosabasut will be alive again. Maybe when the whitemen left with her he became whole again. He was one of the tall men. And wasn't he also a shaman as some said he must have been to bring back caribou for the starving People?

While she is thinking of her People she doesn't fall. This plain is wind-driven hard. The tracks take her to the riverbank. She can see where they bump across the wide ice.

But the tracks aren't where they were this afternoon. Already this river-ice has shifted. She loses them, finds them, loses them again. The moon gives her directions.

On the river travelling is easier. Before pushing into the bush again, she pauses. How far has she travelled? Not enough to stop.

The night cold has firmed the crust. Amongst the trees she begins to move faster, more confident. Suddenly at the bottom of a slope the snow cracks like ice. Snow smothers her like water. In the deep hole she gathers her pain. Sharp crystals catch in her throat. In her hair like grit. She scrabbles out of the white grave. Her legs tremble. Under a spruce she sits. The moon too has fallen. It sits on the horizon, staring at her through the tangled forest.

She cries again. Deep sobs that strain her bruised ribs. Her arms remember Waunathoake. Her hurt breasts remember her. Wau-na-tho-a-ke! Wau-na-tho-a-ke! Then she calls No-nos-a-ba-sut! But more softly.

The moon sinks.

The sun rises.

They find her. They carry her to the sled in a beaver-robe.

The old man walks beside her where she lies on the sled. Now she knows who this oldman is. He is the owner of the house and the boats. This is the man the People watched. This is the man who killed her own mother and many others of the People in the old days. He is grey and cold.

Beside her on the sled are several of his steel traps, grinning like bearjaws. This oldman, Wothamisit said, had killed Wothamisit's brother many years ago when his brother lay in his mamateek crippled from a fall. At the sound of gunfire the others had fled. And alone in the mamateek there, sitting on his rump to defend himself, he'd been battered to death with one of the oldman's traps that the People had taken to make spearheads from.

Trees pass over her as they go. She can't tell where the birchtwigs end and the sky begins. Thick branches fountain into finer and finer ones until they penetrate the air.

And the air too becomes more and more solid, becomes the twigs, becomes thickening branches, rooting itself, finally, in the trunks of the forest.

Every line of Waunathoake's face. Shape of her fingers. Set of her firm tiny feet . . . .

Nonosabasut. His face will not smile for her. She sees it stiff with hate as in life she never knew it.

On her back on the sled. Bone branches fence the sky. She cannot turn away. They have tied her for the nighttime.

This time when she cries her tears drown her eyes until they spill as she twists her head one way or the other way. They melt down her cheeks. Eventually they trickle into the lining of her hood and dampen her coat.

Never. Never again see Nonosabasut. And Waunathoake?

Those foundering cobbles where, old Wothamisit told them, many canoes were smashed in the old seal-hunting days. Under thick snow they seem smooth. On the clifftop juts out stark the birch Nonosabasut climbed to watch the whitemen load their boat.

In the whiteman's mamateek it's very warm. The women in the huge mamateek frighten her. The Micmacs often leave the torture to their women. Maybe the whitemen, friends of the murdering Micmacs, do also. When the women reach to touch her face and finger her clothes she clings to the red-haired one.

She clings to him and calls his name. Johnpeyton! Johnpeyton! At this the women laugh. Behind them, one of the furriers lurking in the doorway makes a joke his fellows snigger over. An old woman flies at the furrier and pushes him outside. She slams the door.

Old man Peyton sits silent brooding over his old man's pains, his old man's memories.

The fire is kept somehow in its own stone house made of cobbles from the shore. There's no smoke from this fire in the whiteman's mamateek. The fire is at one wall, not in the middle where people can sit around it equally. From cruel black hooks large pots dangle. Small pots sit on a flat place by the flames.

One woman tells her SIT. A CHAIR is a thing made of cloth and wood. John Peyton pulls one over for her. It's soft and its arms enclose her.

Three women, dresses all the same, come into the room, then go out again.

She tries to unlace her moccasins. Her fingers are too

swollen. John Peyton draws them off her numb feet. In
the heat her toes throb. Her ears begin aching. Her feet
rest on a bright cover on the floor. Tired. Her eyes close.

There's giggling behind her. She turns towards it. The
three women are staring from a doorway.

The old woman tells them GO AWAY. The door squeaks
shut. Why are these other women dressed alike? Why
are they kept away? She's glad they are kept away because
they frighten her. She's too tired to make sense out of it.

Then one of them comes in again. She gives the men
bowls, hard like metal but with colours on them. She
gives her one too. It's a kind of stew. She goes to drink it.
They all laugh. They are using a metal SPOON. The old
woman pushes it into her hand. But it's too slow that
way. She picks meatchunks out with her fingers.

The heat makes her dizzy. Old man Peyton talks. He
says MARCH. Then, MARY. Then, MARY MARCH. That
pleases everybody. They point to her and say MARY
MARCH MARY MARCH.

The old woman calls JESSIE! One of the three women
comes in, hands stuck in an apron. The old woman
orders her, TAKE MARY, and, UPSTAIRS. A sudden fire
catches a small taper in Jessie's fingers. She touches the
flame to a shiny object on a table. A light blooms. Jessie
carries it, this fire, in her hand and with the other pulls
her to follow.

They climb. One step, then another. Like ledges in the
mamateek but many made of wood, and one built on
top of another. She is much taller than Jessie. She bends
low after her into a small room with a sloped ceiling like

a mamateek. Jessie shows her BED. And at its end a
large BOX.

She won't let Jessie take her coat and put it into the box.
Jessie says OH ALRIGHT. Then she shouts downstairs. The
old woman answers. Jessie pats the bed. TO SLEEP ON.

Under the bed is a dark space. She crawls under there
where it is safe.

Jessie shouts NO MARY. Then Jessie giggles and runs
from the room excited. Downstairs she hears them all
laughing. Then they all come up and peer under the bed
at her, trying to make their light shine where she lies.

Then they take their fire with them and go. Darkness
at last and silence.

She lies. She waits. A square of light falls on the floor.
Where does that come from? She crawls out to investigate. In the wall is an opening. What is it this whiteman's mamateek sees through this eye? But this eye blurs
everything. Ice blinds it as old eyes go blind and change
to white stone. She scrapes at it. The ice melts in her
hand. Then she can see through it as if it were her own
eye. The ground's far down. She can see beyond the
beach the flat stretch of ice that holds the bay. She must
escape soon. But not until she gets stronger and can
gather supplies. She will have to be wise and wait. Besides, they have done something to the door so she can't
move it.

She lies on the bed. But its softness disturbs her. She
lies on the floor instead. This then is the white people's
mamateek which they call HOUSE. A place for the fire. A
special room to sit in. A different place to sleep. Large

boxes where things are hidden so you have to remember where they are. And parts of the house where some people are kept separate from others.

Somewhere else she hears John Peyton, old man Peyton and the old woman arguing. A door slams hard. A baby cries. Their noise disturbed it.

Its wailing goes on and on. It too in its separate room? She doesn't hear a mother come to comfort it. She listens till it stops. Night and the cry together make whole the divided house as she lies there.

Then she, Demasduit, wife of Nonosabasut, mother of Waunathoake, in her belly her own sadness heavy and unuttered, sleeps, for the first time, alone.

REVEREND LEIGH.

She gives Reverend Leigh her hand as she has learned to do. Reverend Leigh is nodding to everybody, answering YES YES? YES YES? YES YES?

When he speaks to her he rests his hands on her shoulders and looks close into her face and says MY CHILD MY CHILD MY CHILD.

She tries to keep close to John Peyton.

They go into the special room for visitors with its high soft chairs. On the walls are pictures of other houses and flowers and animals called SHEEP and COWS. These animals live in ENGLAND which is the special place old Mr and Mrs Peyton came from, Jessie the MAID told her. There is a picture of old Mr Peyton's ANCESTOR, too. Then there is a picture in a heavy frame of KING GEORGE. He has shiny metal on top of his head and chains over his shoulders. But he must be from another tribe in England because he isn't part of Mr Peyton's family.

They eat CAKES and drink TEA. When the fire gets too hot, old Mrs Peyton sets a small embroidered cloth hanging from a metal frame onto the small TABLE between Reverend Leigh and the fireplace so the fire's heat won't touch his face. The same way the People sometimes shield themselves with bark stuck in the floor of the mamateek in winter.

Reverend Leigh pats the seat beside him. COME HERE MARY. COME HERE MARY MY CHILD. Jessie pushes a chair over for her.

Reverend Leigh shows her a BOOK. He opens it and looks and begins to talk in a strange voice. Is this ceremony language? He keeps his eyes down as she remembers the shamans sometimes used to do when they sought guidance from the People's gods. Then everyone in the room puts hands together. They close their eyes as if in a trance and they all say words together, then AMEN AMEN.

There is a word they use when they talk about her. PAGAN.

Reverend Leigh is going. Outside wait two of the white people's animals that are like deer but have heavy feet and no horns. They are pulling a large sled with chairs on it. She has seen these animals from a distance before but never so close up. They have beautiful hair over their necks. Sometimes they make a strange noise that carries like a stag's call in autumn.

Then she sees they are bringing down the box from the end of her bed where they have made her put all her things she was wearing when she arrived. They begin taking it out to the sled.

Her coat is in there. Without her coat there will be no escape until the warmer weather. She runs after the box. GO WAY NO! GO WAY NO! JOHNPEYTON! JOHNPEYTON!

He comes from the special room for visitors. She clings to him. NO GO WAY BOX JOHNPEYTON. He holds her and looks into her face. There's trouble in his eyes. And now he speaks quickly with his mother. She says FOOL! SILLY! Her eyes looking everywhere for servants.

She calls old Mr Peyton. He comes slowly. He has been unwell. He shakes his head at John. NO.

John's red face flushes angry. She clings to him closer.

His mother pulls her away by the hair.

He tells her LISTEN MARY. YOU GO. REVEREND LEIGH TOO.

Jessie brings her a heavy coat. She says YOU GO TOO JOHNPEYTON. GO TOO.

Because she won't wear the coat they have brought her they take her own coat out of the box. They put the box on the sled. She goes through the wet snow with them. They wrap her in a fur-robe.

Reverend Leigh is smiling and saying MY CHILD MY CHILD.

When the HORSES pull, the white people all wave and smile GOODBYE GOODBYE.

John Peyton is the first to turn and go back into the house. . . .

THE LORD BE WITH YOU.

She answers AND WITH THY SPIRIT.

LORD HAVE MERCY UPON US.

She answers CHRIST HAVE MERCY UPON US.

Reverend Leigh tells her VERY GOOD MY CHILD.

Then he tells her that THE GOVERNOR will be pleased to see how quick to understand she is. The Governor is someone like King George. But even he isn't really a member of King George's family. The Governor lives a long way off by big ship in a place called ST JOHN'S.

Then they set to do DRAWING. Reverend Leigh wants her to draw the huge mamateek, the CHURCH that Mrs Hunter took her into yesterday.

She draws the front part where all the people go in.

Then she draws the doors opening and draws how the people sitting in lines are singing and looking at the CROSS at the front.

Reverend Leigh can't understand her drawing even though she tries to tell him the story of it. He takes paper and draws the church too. But he only draws how it looks from the outside as if you were a long way away. It has a huge tower on top, higher than she remembers it and the doors he draws are much smaller than hers.

Also he doesn't draw the doors opening and doesn't show the people singing inside the church. But then Reverend Leigh went into the church a secret way round the back so he might not know how it felt to go through the large front doors and see all the people in lines with their backs to her suddenly all turning and looking and whispering among themselves, small books falling CLAP CLAP off their laps onto the floor.

Reverend Leigh's servant, Mrs Hunter, kept pulling her sleeve to show when to kneel down and when to stand up. Reverend Leigh must be an important man because all the white people came to hear him tell stories in the church.

And the white people knelt and stood keeping their eyes either up or down away from him except when he told a long story, occasionally reading from the book. And then they all looked straight at him except for some old ones and some children who closed their eyes and seemed to be asleep. There was no laughing and clapping and dancing as there was when old Wothamisit used to tell his stories.

Now it is bedtime because CLOCK strikes. This shiny little god is like the one they found in the whiteman's clothes in the boat. It is bigger than that, though, and more powerful. Reverend Leigh listens to it strike. Many times a day he asks what it says and makes sure every day to take care of it with one of his KEYS, sometimes moving the HANDS on its FACE.

Drawing is over. Everyone gathers together. They all kneel down in front of the fireplace. Clock looking down over them and Reverend Leigh making a chant again. In the middle of it he places a hand on her head, and eyes closed, he says AND ESPECIALLY YOUR CHILD MARY MARCH.

Once she is left alone she goes to her box and takes out her coat. Then she takes a piece of bright cloth John Peyton gave her a few days ago when he came into the SHOP where she was with Mrs Hunter.

Instead of dividing their food and their tools one man has it all in a shop. And the man in the shop gives it out to the people in exchange for some bright metal MONEY. Many of the things the people get in the shop are brought to them by big ships from England. These ships fly coloured FLAGS. THE UNION JACK. Mrs Hunter took her to see them.

When John Peyton saw her in the shop he said HOW ARE YOU MARY? I HOPE YOU ARE WELL. Then he took the bright SCARF and gave it to her. When he left he told the shopkeeper, LET HER TAKE WHAT SHE WANTS.

She brings the things from the shop carefully out of the trunk: sixteen SPOONS, sixteen KNIVES, sixteen RIB-

BONS, sixteen THIMBLES, sixteen small pearly BUTTONS, STUDS on a card, a ball of LACE, sixteen HOOKS for catching fish, sixteen spools of COTTON, a small brass KETTLE, and a handful of TOFFEES.

She places everything in the scarf John Peyton bought her. Her NIGHTDRESS, SLIPPERS, CAMISOLE and HANDKERCHIEF, as well as her BONNET and her GLOVES. She ties the bundle. Then she dresses in her own clothes, her coat on top and her moccasins laced firmly.

Then she takes the cooked eggs she has hidden every day under the bed, as well as some sweet rich cake. A bad season to travel, ice breaking up everywhere. But if she's lucky it will hold a few days and then it will be only a half growing of the moon before she will be back with Waunathoake and her own People. She mustn't wait any longer. Soon they will be taking her to the Governor. And the Governor, Mrs Hunter has told her, lives a long way away . . . .

She's left it too late. It's open water to the mainland. Not a chance of crossing it. Nowhere does the ice bridge it. On the shore a pile of sponge-ice is growing in the moonlight. Drizzle pats her face.

The current's force lifts the sponge-ice pile, shoving more ice under it. Tinkling pieces, riddled with sunholes, tumble down its crystal sides. At sunrise or soon after, these new blocks will melt as fast as they are replaced and the pile will not last long after that.

The hush keeps her. She sits. Heavy hands of snow on the low hill's sides squeeze water through the stony ground. The hands of snow grow smaller as they squeeze. They'll disappear themselves into the moist earth soon.

The whole earth murmurs under its lightening white burden. The ice, turning and churning, dissolves as the sea shakes free, and waves slap shore once more. The drizzle turns to hail. On bare rocks it bounces, tiny beads dancing and buzzing like sandfleas in autumn.

THIEF IN THE HOUSE.

Mrs Hunter has been saying WELL DEAR ME REVEREND, WHERE CAN IT BE?

At last they do what their glances have been telling her. They search her room. Mrs Hunter looks under her bed. Not there. Then they open her box.

WHAT ON EARTH ARE THESE?

One pair after another they bring them out. All made of thick blue cloth. All different sizes. Sixteen pairs of well-sewn moccasins.

SO THAT'S WHERE IT WENT.

They accuse her. She remembers, *Let her have what she wants.* She says JOHNPEYTON, JOHNPEYTON.

NOW DON'T BE HASTY MRS HUNTER. JUDGE NOT LEST YE BE . . . .

WHAT ABOUT THESE THEN REVEREND?

MY SILK NIGHTCAPS! WHAT'S SHE DONE WITH THEM? THEY'RE ALL CUT TO SHREDS.

NO NEED TO LOOK FURTHER FOR THOSE ANYWAY REVEREND.

LET'S NOT BE TOO HARD ON THE CHILD MRS HUNTER. MARY MEANT NO SIN I'M SURE.

BUT WHAT IF IT GETS TO SILVER REVEREND? THAT'S QUITE A BOLT OF MY BLUE MATERIAL SHE'S STOLEN THERE. A BAD EXAMPLE TO THE REST OF THE HELP TOO IT IS. SHE'LL HAVE TO LEARN RIGHT FROM WRONG LIKE EVERYONE ELSE.

ALRIGHT MRS HUNTER. YOU DO WHAT YOU THINK BEST. WHAT YOU THINK BEST. YES YES. SHE SHOULD BE TAUGHT. YES YES. MOST CERTAINLY.

Mrs Hunter takes her downstairs. She makes her throw the blue moccasins and the silk stockings she's made into the stove fire, one by one.

The ship was like a house that floated. On shore now. Her legs have grown used to the pitch and roll. But this earth is still.

A crowd gathers. She and Reverend Leigh follow TWO OFFICERS. Up a steep stone path. TO THE CARRIAGE.

Awkward climbing into it because her lace dress tight with STAYS won't let her bend. Her own coat is over the dress. Children rush to touch its painted stencilling. One small girl is dark-eyed dirty, bare feet on cold stone. She turns to hug the little girl, but the quick body twists from her fingers, frightened, and disappears in a doorway.

Their carriage spins round, wheels thunder, hoofs like metal pots clank on the cobbles. Over her, houses, close side by side, dangle from their cliffs. Up. Ship, its tall mast, Union Jack, neat decks below. Up. Slate grey roofs of houses, chimneys breathing smoke, bright gardens here and there. Up. Turn. The town tilts through the curtained carriage-window.

They cross to the cove's far side where a bluff cuts sheer. A stone grey house, stonewalls. A pole. A high-flying flag. Over the stonewalls jut black round mouths. From one, smokewisps ... CAAARRRROOOOMMM ... RROOOOMM ... OOOMM ... shudders the earth. She gasps. Reverend Leigh says DON'T WORRY MY CHILD. SIGNAL HILL. IT'S HIGH NOON. He glances at POCKETWATCH.

At first it seems the band of men have spears. Then she sees they have guns with knives attached. Dressed all the same, they step the same. Red. And their rhythm frightens her.

Past the hill the carriage stops. John Peyton opens the

door for her. Reverend Leigh helps her down as if she were a white lady. HOME.

Mrs Leigh wearing a tall hat is there to greet them. HELLO JAMES. SO THIS IS MARY IS IT? Careful of her hat she gives her husband a Christian greeting.

John Peyton, maintaining his usual forest quiet, stands apart.

She breaks into it. YOU GO SHORE JOHNPEYTON WHEN GO SHORE NO EMAMOOSE FOR YOU LIKE REVEREND LEIGH EMAMOOSE. HA HA HA.

Mrs Leigh laughs. STILL UNWED THEN JOHN? WE'LL SEE WHAT WE CAN DO ABOUT THAT SINCE YOU'LL BE IN ST JOHN'S A WHILE. . . .

Drawing again. This time in Reverend Leigh's REAL house, not his MISSION house. Drawing in the DRAWING ROOM. Mrs Leigh is FAMOUS for her CUSTARDS and her NEEDLEPOINT.

LOOK MARY. Reverend Leigh is drawing. NOW MY CHILD YOU SEE? THIS IS A BOAT AND THESE ARE THE MEN OF HER CREW. AND THIS IS MARY IN THE BOAT. He draws waves. SEE THE BOAT WITH MARY GO UP THE RIVER. THEN STOP. SEE IT STOP BY THIS MAMATEEK. THEN, he winks at Mrs Leigh, THE BOAT COMES BACK AGAIN WITH MARY . . . .
NO NO NO!

She takes the pencil from him and alters his drawing. She leaves herself out of the boat. She draws herself instead standing by the mamateek. She stands by Osnahanut and Shawnadithit. She rocks Waunathoake in her arms. Now it's summer on the peninsula where they stay with Longnon's People. Already the ponds are crowded with waterlilies. She's standing at a place where Nonosabasut saw the fires that morning and thought it might be the whitemen come to avenge the taking of their boat. She stands in the buzz of summertime with Waunathoake in her arms and the sounds of the People busy behind her, chattering, and she listens to the riverrun . . . .

YES YES YES! GOOD FOR MARY!

Reverend Leigh smiles at her and nods.

This morning she woke on her back with legs widespread, floating. Now the dream had made them loose she noticed how tight for months had been the muscles of her thighs and buttocks. Her nipples had sprung like crocuses. But the weight between her legs that had given her the heart-beating dream of a man inside her was just the comforter heavy with the cat, asleep in its warm puddle, purring as she moved and roused it.

When John Peyton came later with cheerful HELLO MARY! she was angry and afraid to stand near him. With an urge to touch trees, frantic, she went to the walled garden. In morning mist, stones smelled of mint.

A gardener's workcoat hung on the handpeg of his oiled scythe. Its sweatsmell caught in her throat. She went dizzy to her knees. Reek of the nearby outhouse assaulted her nostrils, in her ears the caught blue buzz of flies. The mealy earth pressed against her palms. She rocked remembering the forgotten uses of her body.

Reverend Leigh and John Peyton were whispering behind her in the doorway. They would think she was praying.

She hurried back to bed, undressed, and curled like a child into the middle under the covers.

Is this really the body of Demasduit? These last months she's put fat on like a beaver. Her body feels different. Even her hands as they move over and over it begin to feel . . . like someone else's.

WELL WELL MY DEAR CHILD. ARE YOU FEELING POORLY THEN?

WE'VE COME TO SEE HOW YOU ARE MY DEAR.

Mrs Leigh pulls the curtain across a dark window. What has happened? Her bedsheets are soaked through. The lantern the maid holds burns her eyes. Their voices smoke across her blurred room. Then their words flare in her ears.

I THINK SHE'S A LITTLE UNDER THE WEATHER JAMES. TELL HER THE GOOD NEWS AND SHE'LL FEEL BETTER.

MARY MY CHILD YOU'RE TO BE GOING HOME SOON. THE GOVERNOR HAS ORDERED IT.

SHE DOESN'T UNDERSTAND JAMES. TELL HER AGAIN.

HOME, MARY. GOING HOME TO SEE YOUR BABY, MARY. GOING HOME MY CHILD.

If she moves her head she'll fall off the cliff. She presses against the cliff. Too deep a breath, and she might fall off. Below her are all the houses that have already fallen off. And there's a ship that has fallen off. She clings to the mamateek that shelters her People. They don't know it is falling off too. She can feel it begin to go under her, falling, she's falling....

WON'T THAT BE NICE MARY?

OH DEAR, MISSUS. HER HEAD'S REALLY QUITE HOT. FATHER FATHER, IN THY MERCY WE BESEECH THEE....

HURRY JANE. BRING ME SOME WET TOWELS.... BRIGHT AS A NEW PIN TOMORROW... SHOULD HAVE REALIZED THIS MORNING SHE WAS....

... DIDN'T SHOUT BOO FROM BEHIND THE STAIRS AS SHE USUALLY....

... WAYS ARE MYSTERIOUS MY DEAR.... CIVILIZATION

THAT DOES IT . . . CAN'T MIX. THAT'S THE SIZE OF IT, POOR THINGS.

Cool cloth on her forehead. They've taken away the light. No hurts now. Swimming cool. Yes yes. GOOD FOR MARY . . . .

The great boat had creaked. Every roll of it pressed the railing against her hip. A changeable day. She kept watching for any of the People on shore. Places where they would likely be, juts of shingle where a canoe could land but a whiteman's heavy boat couldn't, were all deserted.

No other signs either. She looked for cloth tatters in trees, piles of split shells at the bush edge, debris from the seal-hunt at the tidemarks.

When they reached the full cup of the bay where the People's river discharged itself, John gave her a SPYGLASS. She lifted it. Cliffs leapt close. She moved it slowly. A fox.

He ran the mossed peat blanket on top of the crags, stopped, tilted his nose up to look at the boat, stared full into her eyes. His winter coat was fluffed by the breeze. He sprang away again. His run, she could see, was unnecessarily bounding and jaunty. It was spring.

It is three days since she saw the fox who had made her laugh. That evening she had fallen down again. Now she is lying in bed in the cabin. Every movement of her own is pained and dull. Captain Glascock's brass things lie around her. He has given her a CHART. John Peyton showed her how to look at it. Keep it this way. The chart is like her drawings but the places where the People usually stay are drawn too small on the chart and are difficult to recognize. She drew for Captain Glascock the way the river ran, and made those places where the People stayed large so that he could see them easily. But he had been unable to understand it and had shaken his head, laughed, then gone away.

Because the places where the People stay are very small on this chart she's not sure, sometimes, where to put her markings. The captain has given her a red pencil.

The aching in her head makes her eyes squint. Every morning when she wakes her sheets are wet and smell strangely. Every night fever visits her, bringing her the coughdemon's lurid dreams.

She's hot again. She kicks the sheet off and lies naked in cooling air. Yesterday she was cold and had to put on those flannels Mrs Leigh insists on her wearing.

John Peyton and Captain Glascock left in the CUTTER three days ago, just after she fell. They went up the People's river to make a SURVEY and to see if there were any new mamateeks at its mouth this year.

She had said, JOHNPEYTON. PEOPLE NO COME BY ISLANDS IN BAY THIS YEAR EVER.

He told her they would be going up as far as the first waterfall, then would trek a day in the woods. Flies would have been thick for them because of the warmth of these three days they've been gone. And if some of her People had come they'd be frightened by the Captain and his men and the guns they carried with them.

She should have roused herself and gone with them. Next time she will rouse herself. But that day she had been frightened by the pains in her legs and she couldn't hear well because of the buzz of the fever. She's much better today. If she can only see Waunathoake, rejoin her

People, the living in summer will be easy and she will grow better again. How they'll love the presents she'll bring them. *Oh Demasduit! Look! Look!*

Demasduit. To hear her real name again. She'll get them to say it over and over. Everyone will say Demasduit, Demasduit, Demasduit and leap three times for her. She stretches out her hands. They hold her hands, then they hold each other all together, and she will be Demasduit again. That very same night when they hold her the coughdemon will leave her, and leave Waunathoake too, and she will be happy with the People. Except she will remember Nonosabasut. They will take her to the grave of Nonosabasut, her husband, and she will make a long ceremony for him as his wife should do, and wear grit in her hair until his spirit is peaceful. . . .

When she wakes the cutter has returned. She lies in the evening light on her sweat-wet bed. Cool. Oars thump as the crew stacks them in the cutter. The capstan groans, davits squeak. She pictures how the cutter will be swinging where it had swung before, come back now to its familiar resting place.

Their voices disperse. She waits.

There's John Peyton's step. He taps once, twice. She doesn't move or speak. He opens the door. He looks at her, at her nakedness, hesitates, stays.

Let him look at her. No Mrs Leigh to cluck and insist she cover herself.

He closes the door behind him but stays holding the handle. He gazes at her thin body.

YOU NO FIND MARY'S PEOPLE JOHNPEYTON? AND FLIES

EAT YOU? YES YES. JOHNPEYTON GOOD MAN JOHNPEYTON.

Her tears tire him completely. He slumps against the door and rubs his face in his hands. The flies have chewed him badly. And he is thinking of his once-cruel father, old man himself dying. He's thinking of what his father has done to her People these many years. And then this last thing . . . .

PEOPLE GONE TO LIVE ON RIVER AT LONGNON'S PLACE JOHNPEYTON. SEE. MORE UP RIVER. YOU TAKE ME IN BOAT SOON JOHNPEYTON PLEASE?

She holds the chart for him to take. He stays where he is. His eyes suddenly grow empty, his swollen red face turns redder.

I'LL TELL THE CAPTAIN. YOU REST NOW MARY HEAR? YOU GET BETTER QUICK.

YOU SEE ME IN MORNING JOHNPEYTON PLEASE. NO GO WITHOUT SEE MARY?

AYE. His voice is breaking. AYE . . . DEMASDUIT.

The door opens and shuts like the flicking of her eyes. Chilly now. She pulls up the bed-quilt.

A coughdemon jumps down her throat. She spits him up again. He hides in shadows waiting.

She thinks of the cutter rocking. The sea begins rocking her also.

So long with the white people she may be tainted.

Just to talk with her People then. Just to hold her Waunathoake. How tall she would be now. Maybe she would grow to be one of the tall People like Nonosabasut.

Listening for the coughdemon's shuffle . . . she stays . . . wary . . . .

His Majesty's Sloop Grasshopper
In Peter's Arm, River Exploits.
10th March, 1820.

Sir Charles Hamilton, Bart.
Commander in Chief &c.

Sir,

My letter of the 8th of October stated up to that period the progress that had been made in preparation for wintering at this anchorage; and that Your Excellency may be put in the earliest possession of the more prominent events that have since occurred, I avail myself of an opportunity of conveyance to Fogo to state with brevity such particulars only as seem necessary to convey a general outline of my proceedings.

It was not until the 25th of November that I received Mary March, the Indian female, conducted hither by Mr John Peyton Jr and notwithstanding that my first interview in August led me to conclude that she was in delicate state of health, I could not but grieve to see the progress that a rapid decline had made in the interval, and I observed that she had imprudently thrown aside the flannels which during the summer she wore next her body, and was otherwise thinly clad. Warm dresses were now provided for her and a woman to attend carefully on her; it however soon became too apparent that even should the skill and great care of the surgeon protract her existence through an inclement winter, it was utterly impossible that she could be in a state to travel into the interior; it therefore became a matter of much solicitude to commence the journey as soon as the weather would permit with the view if possible of opening a communication with her countrymen, and of inducing some of them to accompany me to her, as a meeting must in its consequence have operated most powerfully towards effecting the desirable object of producing to those poor creatures the blessings arising from civilization, every preparation was consequently made. She often would express to Mr Peyton and myself that we should not find the Indians, and said "gun no good" but would never hear of us going in without her, at the same time giving us to understand that she only wanted her child and that she would return with us. Nature gradually sunk, but she always continued cheerful until the 8th of January, when she suddenly expired at 2 p.m. A few hours before she had been looking over the track of my former journey which I had frequently got her to do, and which she latterly understood, and took delight in speaking of the wigwams. A short period before her death she was seized with a sort of suffocation, and sent for me and Mr Peyton who had that morning gone for a walk, she soon recovered and appeared as usual, but I had not left her more than a quarter of an hour when being again summoned, I hastened to her and beheld her lifeless, her last wish appears to have been to see Mr Peyton, and she ceased to respire with his name upon her lips. She seemed always much satisfied when he was near and looked up to him as her protector. Her mild and gentle manners and great patience under much suffering endeared her to all, and her dissolution was deeply lamented by us.

As the melancholy event had not been anticipated, it left me without instructions how to act, and as it was now out of my power to return to St John's, I considered it still desirable to prosecute the original design, and many reasons determined me to have the corpse conveyed to the place of her former residence.

. . . We at length on the 11th reached the great Pond, a distance of twenty two miles from the second overfall, which we crossed in a NE. direction for five miles, and at three O'Clock arrived at the former residence of our deceased friend. The frame of two wigwams remained entire, the third had been used as part of the materials in the erection of a cemetery of curious construction where lay the body no doubt of the Indian that had fallen, and with him all his worldly treasure, amongst other things was linen with Mr Peyton's name on it, everything that had been disturbed was carefully replaced, and this sepulchre again closed up, some additional strengthening had been put to it this fall. The coffin which was conveyed to this spot with so much labour was unpacked and found uninjured, it was neatly made and handsomely covered with red cloth ornamented with copper trimmings and breastplate. The corpse, which was carefully secured and decorated with the many trinkets that had been presented to her, was in a most perfect state, and so little was the change in the features that imagination would fancy life not yet extinct. A neat tent that was brought for the purpose was pitched in the area of one of the wigwams, and the coffin covered with a brown cloth pall, was suspended six feet from the ground in a manner to prevent its receiving injury from any animals; in her cassock were placed all such articles as belonged to her that could not be contained in the coffin, the presents for the Indians were also deposited within the tent as well as the sledge on which they had been carried, and all properly secured from the weather....

> I have the honour &c.
> D. Buchan. Commander.

# Shawnadithit

*1820*

Two days after Demasduit's capture Waunathoake had died. A small cough, a short spasm, her eyes opening fully so they'd had to close them. When the sleep-house for Nonosabasut was completed they placed Waunathoake there beside him, sewn carefully as he was in birchbark and well ochred. It was a large place raised on poles by the lakeshore to keep out high water and animals. The next year they watched the party of whitemen leave the pine coffin behind. They were afraid because some said the leader of the party was the same man who had led the party up to the lake many years before when the People had to slay the hostages whose heads Doodebewshet had cut off.

In the pine coffin was Demasduit, so the People had placed her, too, in the sleep-house next to Nonosabasut and her daughter.

Then the People decided to abandon the lakeshore, cursed as it had become. They went to live instead not so far downriver as the peninsula where Longnon's People had been living, but at a nearer joining of rivers, the place where so much salmon was caught the autumn of Nonosabasut's death, the same autumn the boat was taken and the whitemen in revenge came and stole Demasduit from her dead husband.

The river that met the great river here flowed out of a long lake. At the north end of this long lake, that fed the river that flowed southward down to the People's river, there was another river which was wide and swampy. Usually it flowed into the lake from the north but many times it flowed the other way. Always in spring it flowed this way and came out to the northern sea in a small bay where no whitemen lived, the place where Longnon and his boy went that year to search for shellfish, the same winter Nonosabasut and Osnahanut brought back caribou for the starving People, the same winter old Wothamisit, last of the storytellers, was killed by the coughdemon.

Because the People had become so few, and had moved away from the great lake, there was no sense keeping up the deerfences. For two years and longer the dwindling People managed by killing as the caribou came and put themselves before them in the forests.

No children were born who lived beyond many days, and many mothers died with their children. Longnon, grown old and brooding after his son's death the year before, would not wake himself to Osnahanut's pleas and plans. Longnon's only daughter, Dojemathu, a strong hunting woman like Shawnadithit, also grew sullen. So it became everyone hunting for himself, and sometimes even hoarding his catch and not sharing it. Old Wothamisit would have spat *Disgusting!*

Now there were only twenty-three of the People left. A hard winter. No caribou were seen at all and the dried salmon sticks had run out. Eating the inner bark of trees had made the People's mouths swell so speech was difficult. Cold attacked and split their sore lips, their skin grew rashed and tender, cuts wouldn't heal but puffed and agonized them.

Ice on the river and the lake was thick and yet so unstable that nowhere could a hole be driven where fish might be found without it freezing over or shifting during the night, cracking off any twigs that had been left to mark it. One of the People froze over his ice-hole. When they found him his hand still clutched his line. When they freed the line and pulled it out, a fish was still on it. It flopped and danced before his frozen eyes, staining the snow red. Then its own eyes were frozen and they were both dead.

The starving People would not eat this fish.

Marten, too, seemed to have abandoned the area, trapped out by the furriers whose marks were seen everywhere. Several lodges of beaver had also been exterminated by them. And no bears, even, could be shaken from their winter sleep by the lengthening days because it was so cold.

At the coldest heart of winter, the People were dwindling quickly. A month later there were fourteen left. Longnon stirred himself and left with his daughter to hunt shellfish at the northern coast as he had done with his son once before. They departed in numbness, only the slight squeeze of their hands to say farewell.

Then Osnahanut gathered his group about him when Longnon didn't return. She, Shawnadithit. Doodebewshet, her mother. And Suauthwedit, Doodebewshet's other daughter, the singing and dancing one. They left the other eight, some old, perhaps that morning dead where they huddled, some hopeless, and three dumb children among them. These People had promised to rouse themselves the following day and go back to the

People's lake. Maybe they should never have left the lake. Maybe their gods were still there waiting for them to return and prosper. Nonosabasut and Demasduit were still there. And Wothamisit. And the spirits of many other good People in past times.

Osnahanut's group struck out on racquets from the place where so much death had come to the People and began their trek northward, the same way taken by Longnon and his daughter.

They followed the river waterway, pulling the toboggan piled high with skins and utensils. The second day was bright and suddenly warm. It was a good sign. They reached the long lake itself and made good time. No wind bothered them and the sun made the tensed ice crack and boom as they traversed it.

The third day, tired by now, they found an empty trap. A little further was a mounding in the snow. It was Longnon and his daughter. Half-buried they had already been ravaged by animals. Both had been shot.

They stripped bark, laid it over them and piled the site high with stones. When they came back they would try to do something more fitting.

They came to more leg traps. At last they saw one with a rabbit in it. They made a meal of it. A little further they found a marten. Once this lake had been noted for its otters. But none had been found for some time.

Shawnadithit was frightened about taking the marten from its snare. Osnahanut was angry because of Longnon.

—I'd like to give a few of the whitemen's necks over

to your knife, mother.

Doodebewshet was just skinning the animal. She said nothing. She began cleaning the skin off with her lower teeth, scraping and ripping the skin over them, chewing the meaty particles, spitting out stringy pieces of membrane, sneezing when the fur tickled her nose.

Suauthwedit began a coughing fit again. Doodebewshet mumbled —She needs a steambath. That will clear her out. And she could do with a good caribou feast too. Weak coward men. Nothing for my knife for months. Look at that Longnon getting himself shot. His daughter too. And where are we women going to get our babies from when all these men have got themselves killed? We'll have to get them from the whitemen or the Micmacs or those Shaunamunks from up north across the narrow sea.

No one replied. Shawnadithit and Osnahanut hadn't been able to build up a baby in nearly five years together. He glared but kept silent. Stupid old bitch.

Shawnadithit said —We should follow the trapline.

She was no longer frightened about taking the animals because a thought had come to her.

Osnahanut said —What? I thought you were scared. Those furriers will give us the same treatment as poor old Longnon and his girl.

—It's not the meat they want so much. It's the fur. Maybe if we leave the fur behind they won't bother to track us down.

—Alright. It'll keep food in our bellies. It looks as if

they're following the river down. But we'll have to keep wary. Mother! Come over here. You leave that skin in the trap, you hear?

Doodebewshet threw it down by the iron jaw. Then she insulted his presence by arguing with him by speaking as if to Shawnadithit, not addressing him at all.

Because of the warm weather they had to slosh through wide puddles. Other times they flogged through slush, keeping to the banks where the river-ice seemed unsafe, passing strings of small ponds and narrow lakes where the river widened.

The traps they came upon had been newly set. They were still empty and the snow around them had been swept smooth by branches to hide racquetprints. Now and again in sheltered places where the snow had fallen only lightly and had not been smoothed by wind or sun, the racquet-tracks were still clear.

But the last trap they found had bitten into the hind leg of a weasel. It writhed frantic as they came up to it. Finally it stopped, exhausted. Osnahanut waited to club it. He didn't want to miss. Deliberately it closed its eyes as he raised his club. Its fine nose sensed the sweet touches of a young spring wind that ran arms wide down the wakening valley.

They couldn't trust the ice on the opening river because of the sudden thaw. In the thickening woods the toboggan became more trouble. Osnahanut propped it against a tree and marked the place with blazes so they could find it on the way back. They shared the small load, leaving Suauthwedit with nothing to carry. Not far now.

Osnahanut knew of an old mamateek they could spend the night in. It had been built many years ago when the People were many and roamed many lands more than the lake and the river.

Suauthwedit had to keep stopping to rest. They arrived late, after sundown. Their mukluks were soaked through, their feet numbed. Some snow had blown into the mamateek. Shawnadithit swept the floor with spruce-boughs. They lit a fire in the old hearth, piled spruce-boughs into the sleeping hollows, and covered them with dried moss from the lining of the walls.

When the sleep-robes were spread, Doodebewshet took Suauthwedit to sleep with her. Suauthwedit curled like a child against her. With a song, Doodebewshet soothed her suffering.

Osnahanut listened to her curious rough voice. The old bitch of a butcher had been coughing herself lately. Wonder she had the breath to sing at all. Bitter old woman. Careful with old women, don't offend them. Doodebewshet certainly had a grudge against most of the men. Ever since, when he was ten years old, they'd chosen her to cut off the whitemen's heads. They'd chosen her because there was no one else who wanted one of his women to be tainted. Because she'd been recently widowed there was no one to stand up for her. And one of the men was red-haired too. They'd said she'd had a fancy for that one.

Shawnadithit held feet with him. They wiggled their

toes together sharing the shocks of their returning lifeblood as numbness departed. Doodebewshet's song droned on then finished.

Osnahanut ran his hand over Shawnadithit's large hip-ledge. He felt the cool muscle of her thigh. She was young. She was alive. As he too was young and alive. Would the eight they left behind keep their promise and rouse themselves? Maybe there would be something to keep them going on the way back to the great lake. The children wouldn't be able to travel much. If there were no children left in springtime there would be no one to be the People when the others died. Why was it he and Shawnadithit could build no babies? Every night they tried. And other times too. The lake, the river, the forest paths, all empty. The mamateeks all empty and decaying like this one. Only the People's spirits would be there as Nonosabasut and Wothamisit and Longnon and the others were still there, still part of the People. But there would be no breathing, hunting person to bear their memory.

—Shawnadithit! Shawnadithit!

—What? What? Why do you have such a fearsweat, Osnahanut?

It was trickling over his chest and from under his armpits.

—Shawnadithit. If all the People die with no children there will be no one to remember our spirits. We will disappear in the ages like birchbark in the fire. Do you realize that, Shawnadithit?

She said nothing. He held her tightly. The fearsweat

poured from him and his heart throbbed. Her mouth was limp when he caught it. She slid under him and spread herself like a fish split for drying. Frantic he pounded himself into her, fighting the darkness, fighting. But at the end it caught him and he cried in her arms like a child, as Suauthwedit had cried in Doodebewshet's arms. Adrift. He was drowning. It was a ghostly wash of stars.

She too cried. But silently, without Osnahanut knowing....

Unmolested they had reached the sea. The bay was still ice-locked but they found places by the corky rocks where wind had driven floes in tilted cracked plates and the salt sea surged up heavily. On one jut of a broken headland they discovered mussels spread in clear water.

They pried open gravelly shells, chewed, swallowed, and cast them, hinged and empty, frozen butterflies, onto the rocks.

They swilled out their mouths with brine. Their sore gums tingled. After a while their fingers felt warm in the water, but the sky clouded, the wash where they probed grew murky, and a chill blew across the strait from the northern islands.

Suauthwedit sat exhausted and trembling. Her lap was filled with shellfish the others had gathered. Osnahanut noticed her but was afraid to leave the job in case a storm overnight piled the ice up.

—You help Suauthwedit back with what we've got, Shawnadithit. Take my knife so you can pry them open more easily. We'll join you later in the old mamateek with another load. Look. See that shoal just out there? That'll keep us for ages. With the tide going out now we'll find plenty.

—Alright, I'll build her a fire when we get there. The storm will be moving in then so the smoke won't be seen by the trappers. As soon as I've got a fire going I'll come back to give you a hand.

She tied on Suauthwedit's mukluks more firmly and laced on the racquets. Her own mukluks were torn and wet where she had waded. Into the hood of her coat where a baby would ride she piled a load of shells. Once into the wood's shelter it was easier for Suauthwedit.

Halfway they had to stop. She sat hugging Suauthwedit while she gasped and coughed. In the dim light she listened to the storm cuff the treetops. The thick pine they rested against trembled. As they felt the weather snap cold again, spruces pulled their branches down close to their sides as do geese with their feathers when they light on water.

Suauthwedit wanted to rest like a baby against her once her spasms were over. But Shawnadithit rose.

—Come on, sister. If the snow catches you, you will sleep forever.

The old mamateek had lost most of its outer bark casing. The moss inner lining hung down like drying pelts. But it was still a windproof place, this house of their ancestors. The clay their ancestors' hands had packed around the chimney hole was still intact. A big fire would be no danger.

With a spruceswitch she swept out all the snow that remained and cleared the ledges. She built the fire and started it with her firestones. The curled birch tinder flared. Did the bark leave ashes? She watched. It burned completely.

They stuck their feet close. For feet, spring was the worst time of year. In heart of winter, snow was dry like sand. She asked Suauthwedit —Who once lived here, do you know? Were they kin to us?

—I don't know, Shawnadithit. Once the People lived everywhere and gathered on the islands in summer.

—Those of us who are alive should try to remember the dead ones or else their spirits will have no resting place.

Scurrying sand with her fingers to define the fire's hearth safely, she found an old knuckle-game counter chipped at one corner. By the fire's light she saw its fine etching. It was a different design from any she knew. She put it into her coat. It bore a dead hand's memories.

—Well. I'll go back now. There are two big stones in the fire, and a dish of water. Why don't you try boiling some of those mussels I opened? The steam will do you good too.

—Maybe in a little while, Shawnadithit.

She left Suauthwedit crouching, holding her knees by the fireside. Outside she laced on her racquets again and took the old path down to the river. The first pale breath of the storm blew over the river. It was later than she thought. Would they have waited for her, or would they have started out hoping to meet her?

Suddenly she was anxious. She took to the river-ice. Careful she kept away from the outer curves where water below flowed the fastest. With two or more of them on the ice it would have been risky, but alone, and with her racquets to spread the weight, the ice held her easily. Now and again she could hear it splinter along the far shore as she passed.

Then she thought she heard cries. Wolves howling? A gale of wind winding down this valley?

It was voices. She began loping, racquets thrumming as she sprang.

Osnahanut and Doodebewshet! They scrambled down the bank and Osnahanut leapt onto the ice. Doodebewshet leaped behind him but slipped. Her load of mussels spilled across the ice like flung pebbles. Two furriers broke from the trees, guns ready.

She yelled to Osnahanut —Mother's fallen! She's fallen!

He was in midstream. He stopped. He turned. The men were almost to Doodebewshet. He flung off his coat and the load of mussels with it. His hand went for his knife at his belt. She had his knife. He hesitated. Then he sprang towards Doodebewshet.

The ice snapped. He sprang back from the edge of the ice. But the whole large sheet tipped with his weight and slid him into the water. The edge he grabbed for broke in his hand. The next edge broke too.

The men had her mother. They all watched Osnahanut struggle. Again he gripped the floe. It held him. Both hands on it now. With his knife he could have reached, pinned it and hauled himself out as she'd seen men do. His elbows were on it, his chest. Then it tipped like a raft. The edge nearest her rose out of the water.

She ran towards that edge and jumped the yard of open water. She landed in a dive. It cracked. She scrambled. It held her. She crawled towards Osnahanut. Her racquets were awkward. He watched her. Hands get his hands. She was reaching when the ice broke.

Surprise on his blurred face as it sank into the eager

river mouth open crying to her. His hair, like eel-grass, lifted in the water and drifted under a downstream ledge of ice and gently away....

What could she do now? Suauthwedit slept. The storm would keep them from tracking her. And by morning there'd be no tracks to follow. She stirred the fire again. What would they have done with Doodebewshet by now? She kept opening mussels with Osnahanut's knife and throwing them into the boiling water. Don't think. Don't think.

Don't think about Osnahanut's tight body snagged under the river-ice, caught there till the river opened and drifted him down to the open sea. She shivered. She boiled more shellfish. As she leaned over the pot her tears fell onto hot embers and hissed there.

She went out for more wood. Snow fell in soft flakes. Reaching for bones of black deadwood that lay in the powder she watched the snowmoths alight on the decorated leather of her coat. Then the heat of the brushwood torch she carried melted them. The uncertain light of her torch scampered shadows round the boles of trees in the forest. She stuck it into a snowbank while she hunted the area it brightened. There was a lot of wood because the ground hadn't been picked over before. Wet. But she'd leave it by the fire to dry.

There were ghosts in the woods. She ran in frightened. Was Suauthwedit dead? She looked closely at her. She held fingers by her nose. Her nose had been bleeding and was crusted round her nostrils. She was still breathing.

Tomorrow she'd have to tell her. When she got back from the river Suauthwedit had been deep asleep and had let the water cool that was boiling the mussels. The fire was embers.

Close to the fire she sat now and began singing softly Nonosabasut's song about the taking of the whiteman's boat. It was a song about him and Osnahanut, and about herself, and it made play with the sounds of their names. What evil had the People done to have all this come upon them these last many years? Wothamisit had often spoken of how evil men were punished by a monster from the sea. That explained the death of many People in the old days when their canoes tipped in storms and they were found drowned. Maybe there had been a great evil done in times long past, before she was born, and that was why her People had been plagued by the whitemen. Weren't the whitemen from the sea, their huge ships with wings like gulls, the monsters that the old stories warned about?

The fire died, flared again as she fed it, died again. Morning lit the smokehole. Suauthwedit was asleep still. The storm was over. In her throat was a great ache. Her back hurt because she had been bent over in a draught all night. Tired. She laid her head close by Suauthwedit's....

Eight People. She herself made nine. The eight People were walking ahead of her. She thought they were walking. They were going by a long route to avoid the whitemen. The children kept saying to her, *When we get there we'll talk to Nonosabasut, and he'll show us where*

*we can find Osnahanut. Then we can all start again.*
They were in high spirits. They turned and urged her on. *Come on, aunty!*

She reached them. But they weren't walking at all. They were all trapped by the legs, unable to move except a step this way and a step that way, scrabbling uselessly in the snow like snared animals. Their smiles were the leering of lunatics. Before she could step back to go her own way, onto her own leg another trap snapped.

—Shawnadithit! Shawnadithit! Shawnadithit!

She woke. It was her mother! Had Doodebewshet cut off the furriers' heads in the night? She leapt over the hearth-dust to the entrance. She shoved aside the bark door. Into the small clearing stumbled her mother. Behind her stepped two furriers, guns at the ready, wary....

*March 1823*
Among reviving sprucetrees of the warming forest snowfields steam in morning sunshine. Everywhere there's a dead wetrush to the river. The river is jammed and broken. Behind her the men, silent, guns drawn, stop.

Their eyes search over her as the sun's eyes search in the melting woods. Under her coat is hidden Osnahanut's knife, in her warm wet palm, hard. If one of them touches her . . . .

They are camped, eating. Frightened by her sister's coughing the men cut shreds from their trapkills and throw it to where she and the others are sitting. Squatting on their toboggan the men toss hardcakes also. She lets these soften in her mouth.

When they rise Suauthwedit cannot walk. She carries her. Doodebewshet grumbles —Wait till the weather's more certain, Shawnadithit. Then we'll escape them. In the meantime don't fall for their tricks. There's something they must want us fattened for. Keep yourself ready.

But the men take turns keeping a nightwatch.

On the third day they reach the People's river. Its ice booms constantly. The river struggles in winter snares. The way is treacherous but the men, becoming friendly, pull Suauthwedit on their sled. Then they've reached the bay, still ice-struck. A morning's pull across, and they make the brook she hasn't seen for years, the place they beached the boat she and Osnahanut and Nonosabasut had taken.

Warm cobbles line the shore blown bare. They lean

on the wind and listen to it roaming. Their wet treads darken the cobbles like shadows. Hours later her eyes search for the clifftop birch. There.

There also the long-watched house. From the house come men to meet them. Curious women flap behind them. Children huddle by their skirts. Suauthwedit rolls in terror from the sled. Wind flailing her smoky hair, Doodebewshet hunches like a cobble herself and growls
—Look to your knife, Shawnadithit.

Shawnadithit herself stands tall and frightened under the loom of the tall house, under the many gazes that inspect her. The wind grips her ankles. A man with red hair comes to speak some People's language to her. *Greetings . . . friends . . . be welcome . . . .* But a sudden blow across the cove tears through his words. His hat flies. Behind her the whole white bay heaves and splits. Plates grate and shatter on the shore. Far out, blue waves break free.

With the ice-jams down the broken rivers, down the broken rivers to the swollen sea, comes hurtling Osnahanut with his gaping mouth. Cold anguish of his soul blows past her as she stares.

Again she turns to face the whiteman's shelter. Door is opened and they move to enter. The wind besets them all, then, equally.

Shawnadithit treads the shingle away from her mother and her sister. Their backs against the cliff they breathe in spring sunshine. They watch men make boats ready in the mildewed sheds. A man shapes wood for thwarts

on a heavy bench. The wood's skin curls onto the beach
as he worries it. Then it is shaped like bone, hard,
smooth, a pinesmell in the air. Wind hustles shavings
across shingle. A dry sound, like crabs.

She begins her scramble up the cliff. It gives way to
her. Its knees are steep. She slips, clutches, holds, climbs
again, rests. A little higher, and the cliff's hands lift her
like a child. She's on its shoulders.

There's no pathway but she leaps from treefall to rock
to clearspace. Unmolested the birch still sways there. She
climbs. In the crooks of branches are still faint ochre
stains. At the height where the birch nods over all the
other branches she sets herself steady.

Outward the sea. The last ice churns in the growing
surf. Regiments of waves march in. From behind the
crumbling headland a huge ship begins blowing its
heavy way across the bay.

Last ice churns in the surf. Last of her People, her
mother and her sister below, cannot see the monster
coming towards them. Their coughing, with smoke from
the grey chimney, drifts up to her.

On the Governor's desk there's a sheet of paper. Someone says —Give her a pencil.

Shawnadithit draws a deer with two strokes, starting at the tail. The assembly applauds her.

Someone else hands her a strip of birchbark. She folds it several times, puts it into her mouth and indents it, turning it corner to corner. Wet with spittle the bark is unfolded by her onto the Governor's green leather-topped desk. Wet, raw, sweet smelling it lies between a marble inkwell and a golden paperknife.

The Governor sees himself on the sweet, wet, curling birch, his silhouette impressed there by Shawnadithit's teeth. Next to it rests a neat square sheet of blotting paper. The blotting paper still shows clearly the reverse imprint of his latest Royal Proclamation.

*June 24th* —Saw the three Indian women in the street. The ladies had dressed them in English garb, but over their dresses they all had on their, to them, indispensable deerskin shawls; and Shawnadithit thinking the long front of her bonnet an unnecessary appendage had torn it off and in its place had decorated her forehead and her arms with tinsel and coloured paper. They took a few trinkets and a quantity of the fancy paper that is usually wrapped around pieces of linen; but their great selection was pots, kettles, hatchets, hammers, nails and other articles of ironmongery, with which they were loaded, so that they could scarcely walk. It was painful to see the sick woman who, notwithstanding her debility, was determined to have her share in these valuable treasures.

Exploits Burnt Island.
July 23, 1823.

To Captain D. Buchan,
H.M.S. Grasshopper.

Sir,

I beg leave to acquaint you for the information of the Governor that I left the three Indian women on the 12th instant at Charles' brook and that they appeared perfectly happy at our leaving them. I called there again on the 14th instant, when I gave them a little boat, at which the youngest was much pleased, and gave me to understand that she should go to look for the Indians and bring them down with her. I am sorry to add the sick woman still remained without hopes of her recovery.

> I have the honour to be
> Sir,
> Your most obedient
> humble servant,
> Jno. Peyton, Jr

— Doodebewshet, I can tell it won't be long now. You squint at me strangely, as Suauthwedit did. Your eyes, I think, have lost me now. I'll hum while I rock you Doodebewshet till you hear no longer. Here are we two alone on the old robe worn bare, on the bare new sand. The sand runs easily through my fingers now it is full summer.

This place where the rivers join. The last place where the People could have been. Nothing. Not even a trace. Did they wander wildly in the woods until the sun dissolved them as it did the snow they must have slept upon? Or build a last fire, those eight, and walk together into it and burn like birchbark in its flames?

Soon I alone will be left to carry the burden of the People's presence in the People's forests. What shall I say when the trees and waters ask me? Where have you lost them, Shawnadithit? Where have you lost your People?

I lost Suauthwedit by the pine from where old Longnon's boy once saw the stag. She whimpered and refused the steambath. She cried to be held by Doodebewshet. We should have buried her, but Doodebewshet forced me to leave her on the sand point. She said, my mother, *Let the gods take her. Let them take her as they've taken everyone.*

Doodebewshet who can no longer see me, hear. Why did you paddle when I told you not to? And now you have broken yourself, old mother. At least you could have let me throw out the whiteman's pots and kettles to make it easier.

All gone, old mother. Every one. A month, now, searching and not a sign of them.

There. Your hand grips me. I rock you Doodebewshet. I wish I could have held Osnahanut so. Can you hear still? Mother?

I've cut the skins of birchtrees silver. On the yellow beach they curl remodelling the trees I tore them from. A whole day's work I reckon. With Osnahanut's knife I'll cut strong roots and split them fine. With this awl I'll bore places for the threads to pass and tighten. And with this ochre I'll do all that's proper for you. And when you are sewn in the sweet birch and the birch is well ochred ready, and my fingers ache, and my throat aches too because of my all-day silence, I'll sing you a song of your People. Of how you were a beautiful woman of the People, and how you bore two daughters who became the last of the People, how you were the mother of one daughter especially, Shawnadithit, who was left behind with no one to sing for her at the hour of her own death, who went unremembered, the last of the People in the whole high land of the long lakes and the speaking rivers that run to the sea forever, bearing no longer the living People through the frogback rapids, bearing only the dead leaves of the woods in autumn. Listen, mother. Listen. This is where the riverrun ends.

*Doodebewshet, Doodebewshet*
*widun widun Doodebewshet*
*odemet Doodebewshet*
*odemet Doodebewshet*
*widun widun ....*

*March 13, 1973*
Shawnadithit (or Nancy as she came to be called) died in St John's on June 6, 1829. She died shortly after taking her leave of the explorer and scholar, William Cormack, who had harboured her for some months in his house at St John's and had questioned her extensively about her People.

When he had to leave for New Westminster, B.C., Cormack asked for a lock of her hair. After much hesitation she gave it to him. Then, sensing her own approaching death, she gave him a large quartz crystal and a rounded piece of granite. Those were from the shore of the People's lake. She also left behind her a few drawings, and little else.

Her grave, originally in the Church of England cemetery on the Southside, St John's, was lost when the cemetery made way for a city street.